Krishna: The History and Legacy of the Popular Hindu Deity

By Charles River Editors

Ang Mo Kio's picture of a Krishna statue at the Sri Mariamman Temple in Singapore

About Charles River Editors

Charles River Editors is a boutique digital publishing company, specializing in bringing history back to life with educational and engaging books on a wide range of topics. Keep up to date with our new and free offerings with this 5 second sign up on our weekly mailing list, and visit Our Kindle Author Page to see other recently published Kindle titles.

We make these books for you and always want to know our readers' opinions, so we encourage you to leave reviews and look forward to publishing new and exciting titles each week.

Introduction

A depiction of Vāsudeva-Krishna on a 2ⁿᵈ century BCE coin

In the West, Hinduism is a religion that everyone has heard of but one that few non-practitioners truly understand. Today it is widely regarded as one of the world's great religions and considered the indigenous religion of India, with practices and beliefs stretching back thousands of years.

However, many of these so-called facts are actually erroneous. Hinduism as it is conceived of today is a conglomerate of a number of indigenous Indian religions; in fact, prior to the migration of Islam and the corporate invasion of the British, Hinduism may not have existed at all. Rather, a number of local religious traditions had very old belief systems dating back hundreds or thousands of years, depending on the tradition, and many worshiped gods that are no longer worshiped today. In essence, it was only through the non-indigenous populations in India, namely the Turks and later the British, who defined what Hinduism was. The British in particular asked only a certain subset of native informants from Bengal "what their religion was" and got a very particular answer, giving rise to the West's perception of a singular religious Indian tradition known as Hinduism. If the British had not centered their investments in Calcutta, they may have asked a different group of Indians what their religion was and received a different answer, thus changing the popular conception of Hinduism altogether. In other words, Hinduism is as much defined by the non-native "Other" as it is by the so-called native.

Hinduism as a religion spans more than 3,000 years, and now it includes nearly 1 billion people. At the same time, it is not a specific term, since there are clear sectarian boundaries, the same way there are differences between Protestantism and Catholicism, and even differences between the various Protestant sects and the various Catholic sects, Hinduism may be broken down into many major sub-groupings that may or may not have much in common at all. Additionally, in the same way Christianity contains many smaller, spirituality heterodox groups like Gnostic Christianity (which are sometimes called cults),

Hinduism also contains many groups that have beliefs that do not fit easily within the common corpus of Hindu belief systems. All of these divisions came well after the time of the Aryans, and Hinduism likely began to divide around the 1st century CE, about 1,000 years after the arrival of the Aryans into the Indian subcontinent.

Sri Krishna, believed to be the eighth incarnation of Vishnu, is without question one of the most popular and instantly recognizable deities within the Hindu pantheon, which encompasses hundreds of Puranic divine beings, coupled with approximately 33 Vedic gods and goddesses or "devas," and a sea of other lower-ranking demigods and legendary figures. The likeness of the blue-skinned, flute-toting god, blessed with an unspeakably beautiful face and midnight-black curls, has been replicated in countless sculptures, often clad in colorful clothes and adorned with gold and silver jewelry, relief carvings, paintings, and other artistic mediums, otherwise known as "murti." Hindus and subscribers of the Bhagavad Gita, as well as practitioners of bhakti yoga, ashtanga yoga, jñana yoga, and karma yoga are intimately familiar with this god of unconditional love, compassion, and tenderness, who has also been crowned "Yogesvara," the master of yogis and all things mystical.

While Hinduism has always seemed complicated to outsiders, even those not terribly familiar with the faith and those unpracticed in the art of yoga know of Krishna, or at the very least they have heard his name in the course of conversation. It is particularly difficult, if not impossible to escape the deity's omnipresence in India. In all likelihood, tourists privileged enough to experience the enchanting republic firsthand have visited (or marveled at in passing) one of the innumerable temples dedicated to Krishna peppered throughout India, and this is excluding the shrines erected in his honor in other parts of the world.

Perhaps it was the Radha Parthasarathi in Anantapur, Andhra Pradesh that caught their eye: a vibrant temple built in the shape of a chariot and painted entirely in the dainty shade of watermelon-pink, complete with wheels and a quartet of colossal stallions that towered over its visitors. Or perhaps it was the Sri Sri Radha Parthasarathi Mandir in New Delhi that stopped them in their tracks: a stunning and sprawling complex dominated by lace-white pointed oval domes and embellished with wooden, marble, and stone lattice carvings, which houses the 1,764-pound Astounding Bhagavad Gita, the "largest principle sacred text ever to be printed." The Vrindavan Chandrodaya Mandir, currently under construction, is slated to be the tallest religious monument ever built. Needless to say, the existence of these shrines alone is proof enough that Krishna is no ordinary divinity.

Krishna: The History and Legacy of the Popular Hindu

Deity examines the religion, Krishna's place in it, and more. Along with pictures and a bibliography, you will learn about Krishna like never before.

The Aryans and the Origins of Hinduism

Long before Muslims or the British came to India, another group of foreign peoples migrated into South Asia and brought with them language and culture that would forever change the face of the Indian subcontinent. These peoples, known as the Aryans, likely migrated sometime around the 15th century B.C., or sometime soon after. When they came, they brought with them a rigid, formalistic priest-based religious system that soon became so tightly ingrained into Indian culture that today it is considered the singular most important and influential religious system in all of India, although not everyone still practices what the Aryan texts preached. The Aryans, of course, brought with them the Vedas, written in a language called Sanskrit. They believed that society should be ordered according to function, with priests on top, a societal arrangement has come to be called the caste-system.

Despite the contemporary stereotypes of what an Aryan is according to the 20th century re-invention of the terminology, an Aryan of 4,000 years ago is not nearly the same as those who are now popularly conceived of as Aryan. Who the Aryans really were is subject to much debate, but it is likely that they came from Central Asia. The term "Aryan" itself comes from the Sanskrit word "arya", which means Noble. This self-imposed label designates how the Aryans saw themselves as elites in every way, including culturally, spiritually, and (presumably) economically. The caste system of the Aryans holds that the bottom rung of society, Shudras, is an extremely impure, dirty, and disrespectable class. Shudras would likely not have been termed "arya" like the upper tiers of society, although Shudras in Classical India (300 BCE - 1200 CE) were known to ascend to Kingly status and/or take up occupations that made them wealthy. Today many Shudras are wealthy because they undertake profitable business decisions, such as trash cleanup, that people from the other castes do not want to engage in. Those on the top rungs of Aryan (also known as Vedic) society often were the first to convert to a rival religion, such as Buddhism or Jainism.

   Sanskrit was the language of choice for the Aryans, and it is an Indo-European language that is related to some modern European languages. In fact, there are many cognate words between Sanskrit and these modern languages. For instance, the word "same" in English is cognate linguistically with the word "sama" in Sanskrit. Modern Hindi developed from Sanskrit but displays many assimilated features rooted in later languages, such as Persian, and words introduced from European languages due to European colonizers and the European cultural impact. At the same time, the transfer of words went both ways; for instance, the English words "jungle" and "pajama" come from Hindi.

   Sanskrit is a conglomerate of two words: sam + krita. Sam means "complete" while krita means "done." In other words, Sanskrit means refined, perfected, accomplished. In the Vedas, Sanskrit was the voice of the gods, and the hymns of the Vedas formed the liturgy and ritual language for sages. Later, at around the turn of the millenium into the Common Era, Sanskrit gradually became the language of the gods, rather than for the gods. In a sense, the Sanskrit language became carefully codified by the grammatical rules of Panini, a great scholar living in perhaps the third century B.C. After most authors became adherents of Panini's style of Sanskrit grammar, classical Sanskrit became the catalyst and carrier of culture throughout South and Southeast Asia.

   Sanskrit is the oldest extant language of its family and is related to English, German, French, and other languages, but over time it had much contact with Persian and Avestan and adopted some words and grammatical constructions from these languages. It is likely that it also absorbed or adopted a great deal of the linguistic conventions that were "native" to South Asia. These languages are known as Dravidian languages, although it is controversial to fully claim any aspect of the relationship between Sanskrit and non-Sanskritic languages of South Asia. All of the languages have a lengthy linguistic history.

After about 1200 years in the Common Era, Sanskrit became extremely concrete and regimented. Authors could innovate with their compositions but had to do so within a tight grammatical construct set forth by Panini. As invaders came into South Asia, namely the Turkish Muslims, and later the Europeans, Sanskrit became a fascinating subject for study, especially for the British. The British studied Sanskrit because they believed it held the key to understanding the natives and could unlock the secrets of how to govern the large mass of land and her native inhabitants. That said, as the British gradually began to understand more and more Sanskrit, they in turn relied more and more on what had been written nearly 2000 years prior. So the Laws of Manu, composed perhaps in the 1st century CE, were enforced because the British thought that that was how the Indians could be controlled. Little did the British know that strict enforcements rooted in these ancient texts actually disallowed many cultural customs from all over India. In one sense, this enforcement did violence to the varied Indian cultural contexts because the British privileged only Sanskrit texts from north India.

The Aryans likely also brought with them new forms of tools, new technologies, new food, and new culture, including religion. The Aryans were a horse people with a well-defined set of their own beliefs, including worshipers of sky gods. Most notably, the Aryans had mystics who recited divine hymns, performed divine rituals, and were users of soma, a divine substance that was believed to make priests powerful with magic and religious ecstasy.

The various belief systems on the Indian subcontinent, like Buddhism, owe some of their belief systems to the Aryans. Priestly soma users eventually collected their orally transmitted texts, which included teachings, stories, songs, rituals, and sacred mantras amongst other things, sometime around the 1st millennium B.C. The earliest anthology known presently is called the Rg Veda, a lengthy hymn known to specific families who were entrusted to memorize, preserve, and conduct the rituals within the text. Rg is the name of the text, while Veda is the so-called category of the text. Thus, when referring to these early Sanskrit texts of the Aryans, they should be called the Vedas generally. Other important Vedas are the Sama Veda, which collects the priest-musician's chants and notations, the Yajur Veda, which collects the words of magical ritual formulas, and the Atharva Veda, which contains rituals and incantations used for combating disease, evil doings, and witchcraft.

Later, the Aryans composed commentaries on the Vedic rituals called the Brahmanas. Another set of texts were called the Aranyakas. These texts contained sacred knowledge which could only be learned while practicing rites and rituals in a secluded forest. A last layer of Aryan texts was composed at or around the time period in which the Buddha himself lived. The Upanishads are a genre of religious literature that ought to be passed on from one teacher to one pupil via oral transmission. To date, more than 100 different Upanishads are known, and in addition to teaching various religious principles rooted in the magical incantations known from the Vedas, they also added new philosophies to the already ancient Vedic knowledge. One such philosophy was that an individual self, called atman, could liberate itself from a world of constantly changing, illusory experiences and join with the unchanging universal One, called the Brahman (not to be confused with the genre of literature known as the Brahmanas, or the priestly caste known as the Brahmins). An individual self, or atman, could attain knowledge of the supreme Brahman only through the secret, sacred teachings from wise gurus. At its heart, this knowledge espoused a saying in Sanskrit which translates to "You are that." (Tat tvam asi). Therefore, the core of these teachings insist that the individual practitioner can attain liberation (moksha) from the illusory world through direct insight that one is already a part of the Brahman, the supreme, overarching cosmic ocean that is forever unchanging.

What the Aryans did not bring with them was Hinduism. In fact, Hindu is not even a Sanskrit word; the word is derived from what the Persians called the people who lived in proximity to and across the Sindhu River, and textual references to the people of Sind date to the first few centuries of the Common Era. Thus, the term Hindu, while still old in and of itself, is not as old as the core religious ideals brought in by the Aryans, which predate the word Hindu by nearly 1,000 years. It would be far later that the term "Hinduism" became commonplace, and at that point it was in reference to all of the religions of India not called Buddhism, Jainism, or Sikhism. Since the term Hinduism only became fashionable during the colonial period of British rule, Hindu as a descriptive word predates Hinduism as a descriptive word by at least 1,800 years.

The Persians were not the first to generically describe all of the people in what is now called South Asia, since the Aryans themselves used a term that is still in use today. The Aryans called everyone who was native to South Asia and not practitioners of the Aryan religion Dasas. In the Rg Veda, Dasas were a generic term used to describe enemies and native inhabitants. Later, in classical Sanskrit culture, the word Dasa came to mean "servant" or even "slave." It is little known that in ancient India there was a slave trade and a culture of servitude that is not discussed often.

However, in modern times the word Dasa, or Das, now has a positive connotation, usually for religious leaders, which means "servant of…" It is not known when the term Dasa became a positive one, since its oldest use certainly had negative connotations, but most of the time today, especially with gurus, the word Dasa will be used in conjunction with the name of a god in the Hindu pantheon, such as Kali. Therefore, the famous Sanskrit poet who wrote Shakuntala, Kalidasa, has a name that literally translates to "Servant of Kali." Indeed, at the beginning of nearly all of his poetic and dramatic works, Kalidasa includes great praises for the great goddess Kali.

Despite this long period of existence, the religion of the Aryans has been reluctant to change and/or give up many of its conservative principles. Society is carefully divided, every natural element is an object of worship, animals are sacred for a variety of reasons and often the object of worship as well, goddesses are ruthless and often considered extremely powerful and dangerous, and many of the most ancient worship practices may pre-date the arrival of the Aryans entirely.

Some scholars wish to date the development of Hinduism back to the Indus Valley period, from approximately 3600-1900 B.C. However, this is only a tentative conclusion since this civilization, whose written records we cannot yet read, pre-dates the proposed composition of the Rg Veda. Additionally, there is little to no evidence suggesting that the peoples of the Indus Valley ever knew about the Aryans or their culture.

  If there is little to no evidence linking the two, why do some scholars reach this conclusion? Much of this awkward historical suggestion can be attributed to a single seal on a piece of clay. Such seals were used as "stamps" on traded goods and have been found as far West as Mesopotamia and Egypt. One such clay seal contains a figure who is seated in a cross-legged meditative posture, which suggests the figure is meditating or at least knows about yogic postures more generally. Called the "proto-Shiva" seal for its likeness to much later iconography of the great Hindu god Shiva, this figure also wears a headdress and has an erect phallus. The erect phallus is also a very typical iconographic representation of the later Hindu god Shiva, whose "lingam" is the object of devotion for several thousand years.

The Swaminarayan Akshardham Temple in Delhi.

The Vedas are the early core texts of Vedic (aka Aryan) religion, and the word "Veda" literally means knowledge, derived from the Sanskrit verbal root /vid (which means "to know")

The earliest Veda, called the Rg Veda, dates to approximately the 1st millennium B.C., while the other major Vedas (the Sama, the Yajur, and the Atharva Vedas) date to sometime after the Rg. Each Veda is a book compilation that covers a different subject, but despite the fact the content is dispersed through the four Vedas, the Rg Veda maintains a more important role in religion over the others. The Rg Veda contains more than

1,000 hymns, most of which are between 5-20 verses (though some go on for more than 50 verses), and it is widely believed these hymns were meant to be sung or recited in a lyrical manner. Most hymns shout praises upon the large number of Vedic gods, goddesses, and divine forms, while also detailing the history of multiple creation stories contained therein.

Manuscript of the Rg Veda in Devanagari, from the early 19th century.

Of the major gods found in the corpus of Vedic literature, few are as important as Indra, the king of the gods who functions very similarly to how Zeus functioned in the pantheon of ancient Greek gods. Indra is lord of the storms and of rain. Another important god is Agni, the fire god, and today the modern Hindi word for fire is simply "Ag". Other gods include Mitra, Varuna, Savitri, Soma, and the Ashvin gods. Most Vedic gods fall out of prominence after the Vedic period but play a behind-the-scenes role in later Classical Hinduism. Sometimes they are even the butt of jokes or the first to convert to new religious sects.

19th century painting depicting Indra

The very popular gods Vishnu and Shiva, who are by far the two most paramount deities in Classical Hinduism, are mentioned in the Vedas but do not have the same iconography associated with them. They also do not serve in the same roles or "divine offices" that they would eventually come to inhabit thousands of years later.

Goddesses play a large role in the Vedic texts. They frequently begot other gods and goddesses and play major roles in creation. The goddess Aditi is the mother of all the gods. Rg Vedic religion is henotheistic, meaning that its polytheism associates supreme divinity in different ways in different texts, whereas Vishnu and Shiva later came to be revered as all-powerful singular god entities. In that sense, as opposed to the polytheism of the Vedic texts, some argue that devotional Hinduism as seen in the Vaishnava and Shaiva movements in the Middle Ages is monotheistic to some extent.

Early 19th century illustration depicting Lord Brahma and Adhiti

The Yajur and the Sama Veda took much of their content from the Rg Veda, but their hymns were organized in different ways to give praise to different gods and godessses. Moreover, these Vedas were very ritualistic, and the hymns were often used to conduct various sacrifices and rituals.

The Yajur Veda has two traditions: the Black and the White. The Yajur Veda are chants which preclude ancient rites, while the Sama Veda chants mostly praise the god Soma, the personification of the soma substance which Vedic priests consumed during ritual activity. Soma was likely a powerful stimulant of some kind that caused hallucinations and dreams.

Public rituals, such as the horse sacrifice (Ashvamedha) were common, especially with kings whose rule must have been consecrated through a divine authority. The Atharva Veda, which came somewhat later, is a compilation of many spells, charms, and wards, and priests would be hired by various individuals to perform these spells, charms, and wards to do everything from acquiring a good marriage partner to bringing the rains for crops. Wards against disease were also incredibly common and powerful tools. Naturally, since the priests were the only ones with the command of the language and knowledge to perform such sacred rites, they were constantly employed, and this remains the case for the most part, although the tradition has certainly changed over the past few thousand years. Even today, brahmins (priests) are required to perform many different types of rituals, like marriages and death rites, The Atharva Veda is the inspiration for the Ayurveda tradition, comprising the science of Indian medicine. Today, Ayurveda is a popular means of holistic health treatment.

The Vedas claim to not have been written by humans and are instead composed of divine revelation as received by seers called rishis. The name of the different rishis who received different hymns and texts can be found at the end of many chants. Rishis, who were a special class of priests, were likely the first to compose these hymns and passed these hymns down orally for thousands of years. In fact, there were no Vedic manuscripts until well into the Common Era, with all of the written texts dating to after the 10th century, making the oral tradition a remarkable achievement of traditional oral culture rarely found throughout the world. To this day, brahmins pass their knowledge on orally.

It was not until Westerners entered India that many texts were first written down. Words and their sonic associations are considered extremely powerful, with the Vedic words being particularly mystical. Vedic Sanskrit is slightly different from later Sanskrit, containing some different grammatical rules and compositional structures, but priests are still expected to memorize all of the Vedas and know about every passage. Given the language difference, this type of study takes an entire lifetime to fully master.

Mainstream Hinduism posits that there are three primary aspects of the Absolute: Brahman, Paramatma, and Bhagavan. The Upanishads described Brahman in detail, with the Bhagavad Gita and other texts describing the lives of godly incarnations that best illustrate the concept of Bhagavan, the aspect of the Divine Absolute which possesses qualities (often human qualities). One might summarize the different between the Brahman and Bhagavan as formless and form. Meanwhile the various systems of yoga describe the Paramatma, the Super Soul. Although tradition differentiates between these three divine aspects, most systems in one way or another describe these three as the "same." In other words, non-dualism of the divine is a popular religious belief, especially for those who are bhaktas, or adherents to the Bhakti Yoga path first described in the Bhagavad Gita by Lord Krishna.

To understand Paramatma, it is necessary to remember atma means "self" and parama means "super." If atma(n) is thus the inner self, which is different from the physical body, it may be described as a type of energy. The atma(n) is eternal, unchanging, and cannot be destroyed.

As one progresses along the path of liberation, one will gradually realize that the Paramatma and the jiva-atman ("individual self") are eternally connected as if they were situated on the same tree like two birds. This relationship is difficult to explain and more difficult to understand. By entering into deep meditative trances known as samadhi, one can gradually realize that the Paramatman is actually present within the jiva-atman. The Paramatman is basically the part of the transcendental Brahman that exists within every individual. Realization through mystical experience or through knowledge is said to be joyous, filling the devotee with complete glee and excitement.

There are also three energies of the divine reality. The first is cit, or the "spiritual energy." With cit, the divine world known as Vaikuntha is created. Vaikuntha is the cosmic spiritual universe where the laws of nature are different from in the material world, i.e. Earth. Cit is the power that allows the Bhagavan, the formed, quality-embracing aspect of the divine, to enter the material world as an avatara, like King Rama or Lord Krishna, but maintain spiritual potency.

Classically, an individual's consciousness does not arise from materiality but rather from the force of individual consciousness known as jiva. Jiva may be better translated as "soul" than atman, which could be better described as "self." Once the jiva leaves a body, so too does the consciousness. Jiva is originally a part of the Brahman but succumbs to the delusion of the material world and forgets its relationship to the Brahman. While under the power of the material world, the jiva, in a body, is subjected to the laws of suffering and illusion, also known as "maya." Thus, liberation only comes to the jiva once it realizes its true state as part of the supreme Brahman. Only through tremendous and rigorous practice, knowledge, and realization can the jiva do this.

Maya ("material illusion") is the reason for the jiva's forgetfulness. Maya can also induce a jiva to not only forget its true nature, but also to believe in false, temporary happiness as it relates to the material world. Desire is a product of maya here. Maya causes the jiva to perform actions (karma) which have consequences, often negative, especially as it relates to the jiva's search for perfection. Maya is often described with the simple metaphor of a rope. If a man is walking at night and sees the outline of a rope on the ground, he may interpret that rope as a snake, which will scare him, even though the rope is just a rope and not a snake at all. Such is maya, an illusion created by the various natural elements of the material world.

The law of karmic causality governs the material world. Simplified in English as "cause and effect," the law of karmic rebirth states that a jiva performing action in the material world is subject to transmigration, causing his "self" to constantly move from body to body. During transmigration, the jiva suffers or enjoys the consequences of his past actions (karma). For the most part, karma is considered to be bondage. A jiva is bound eternally by the action and reaction unless the jiva realizes that it consistently makes its own fate through engaging in good or bad action. Each creates a subsequent reaction.

It is possible, however, to free oneself from this eternal bind. Knowledge is one way. Another is to engage in Karma Yoga, which is not abstinence from karmic activity but rather devoting all action to the yajna, or "sacrifice." In this way, the practitioner performs the action but does not reap or enjoy any of the rewards or suffer any of the consequences. Activity in this mold has been called akarma ("actionless") Bhakti Yoga is described in the Bhagavad Gita as the highest technique of liberation from the material world.

Repeated birth and death, called transmigration in philosophy, has an important Sanskrit name: samsara. Literally meaning "wheel," samsara is the condition of rebirth into various species, of which the texts number at 8,400,000. Being born as a human suggests that the jiva has been born thousands if not millions of times and has cultivated self-realization. As a human, then, one has the ability to achieve liberation, or "moksha," from samsara.

The Wheel of Life, by Stephen Shephard

Three qualities govern samsara and are called the three gunas, or "ropes." These three modes are goodness (sattva), passion (rajas), and ignorance (tamas). The "ropes" actively bind the jiva depending on the actions of the jiva. In the Bhagavad Gita, the rajas, or "passion," guna binds a jiva based on his sexual desire, among other passionate activities including cravings. A jiva's binding may not be entirely dependent on just one of these modes but is usually attributed to a combination of them.

According to tradition, a jiva may actively transcend these binding ropes through devotional activity, sacrificial activity, or pure knowledge.

Beyond these foundational religious principles, many teachers throughout the ages have amended the Vedic religion. Some teachers accept all of it wholesale, while others tend to change or reinterpret certain principles. There are a number of different sub-schools within Classical Hinduism, but explaining some of the examples of opposing schools and philosophies will suffice to explain the breadth of Hindu belief.

First, there is the philosophy of non-dualism, meaning that the cosmic Brahman and the individual atman are actually one single entity. Throughout its history, most major thinkers within Hinduism have subscribed to some form of non-dualism, but there are dualistic schools as well. These terminologies are best described in the original Sanskrit: non-dualism is advaita and dualism is dvaita.

For Advaita Vedanta philosophy, we may turn to the great Shankara, an 8th century Shaiva (devotee of Shiva) brahmin. He wrote many texts and commentaries on famous texts like the Bhagavad Gita, and he postulated that the jiva is exactly identical to God, which is a singular entity. Although it seems like divinity is divided, at its core this is illusion, as divinity is ultimately undivided at all times.

An illustration depicting Shankara

Another major philosopher was Ramanuja, a south Indian brahmin born in the 11th century. He was a Vaishnava (devotee of Vishnu) who taught that there is some difference between the individual jiva and the Brahman. His philosophy, qualified non-dualism (vishishtadvaita), suggests that the Brahman includes things that change (such as the material world and the jivas bound to it) and things that are without change, such as the transcendental God. Implicit in this philosophy is that God controls the material world and the jivas.

Yet another major innovator was Madhva, another Vaishnava (devotee of Vishnu) born in the 13th century. Madhva taught pure dualism (shuddha-dvaita) and argued that there are three cosmic entities: the Lord, the jiva, and the material world. Whereas Ramanuja believed that ultimately the Lord and the jivas were not separate but could be seen as distinct, Madhva argued that they are completely separate. God is a separate entity complete from his creation, the material world. There is a hierarchy' the Lord controls his creation, the jivas can control the material world (to some extent), while the material world is just matter. Madhva advocated bhakti, or complete devotion to the Lord as the primary means of release.

Illustration depicting Madhva

One of the most important philosophers for bhakti religion came in the form of Chaitanya, a 16th century Bengali man who took devotion to Vishnu (specifically, his form as Krishna) to a new level. Chaitanya advocated devotional theism, which proposes a philosophical reconciliation between the Advaitins and the Dvaitins. Chaitanya contended that the jivas and the Brahman are one and the same, but not. His philosophy may be called acintya-bheda-abheda (inconceivable singularity and distinction). For Chaitanya, devotion to Lord Krishna was the most powerful method for freedom from bondage. In other words, Chaitanya formulated a type of personal relationship between God and His devotees. The true meaning of the Vedas is this personal relationship, which may take on a variety of forms.

Sri Chaitanya and Nityananda perform a "kirtan" in Bengal

Classical Hinduism may have developed several complex and interesting philosophical systems, but the primary factor in the worship of everyday Hindus is at the temple, and the belief that philosophy means nothing without an accompanying pragmatic approach to its religious system. Central to the temple culture is the development of what may be labeled classical Sanskrit in the early centuries of the Common Era. Sanskrit dates to well before 1000 B.C., but the Sanskrit of the Vedas is not the same as the Sanskrit language of the Mahabharata or the poetry of Kalidasa. Put simply, the development of Sanskrit as more than a liturgical language allowed new dimensions and forms of religious belief and practice to accelerate and spread.

In the early centuries of the Common Era, Sanskrit became a catalyst of classical pre-modern Indian culture. One of the areas where it especially excelled was in the courtly culture of the time. There, in the courts of kings, philosophers would debate back and forth amongst each other to impress the king. Furthermore, court poets, such as the Buddhist convert Ashvaghosha or the extremely famous Kalidasa, would compose poetry, drama, and other types of entertainment in Sanskrit for the perusal of the king and his court. Quite often these Sanskrit compositions themselves were about courtly life, thus forming a bit of irony for those who were entertained by the compositions.

Sanskrit is also extremely important for Hindu temples. It is there that the old Vedic rituals and sacrifices are performed, but it is also there where mantras are recited, hymns are sung, and sacred scriptures are recited and orated. Some Hindu temples are massive and extremely luxurious, since they house Hindu gods quite literally.

Others are small roadside shrines that are perhaps just makeshift structures. Nevertheless, as Sanskrit grew in importance for kings, so too did Hindu temples, which experienced a great surge of patronage in the Common Era. The Gupta Kings after the 4th century funded the construction of many of the earliest Hindu temples in all of India, and some still stand today.

Typically, communities emerge around temple locations. People need Brahmanical priests to perform life-cycle ceremonies, so they tend to settle where they can gain access to these rites. Over time, temples grew into giant complexes where merchants would set up shops and stalls to sell goods to people coming to worship. To this day, temples serve as an important economic center for communities. During festival times, when there is a huge swell of people, temples, markets, and individual proprietors all experience a great abundance of new customers, which means much more wealth is spread around.

Many private homes contain small shrines inside, and most families associate with one deity or another and thus setup a private space to perform worship to that deity, a practice called puja. At these shrines, or at large temple complexes, it is thought that the gods actually inhabit the stone murti, or "statue." Thus, the murtis are treated as if they were royal guests -- they take meals, they are bathed, they sleep, they see their devotees, and they sometimes provide miraculous occurrences for devotees.

At temples devoted to deities whose practitioners are bhaktas, or devotional devotees, bhakti rituals are performed *en masse*. These often involve singing and dancing, especially as a community, often in the street. The modern day Hare Krishna movement is an excellent representation of this kind of temple culture. Kirtan dancing is an excellent way to not only worship the divine lord but also a great way to proselytize and gain exposure for the temple and community.

Major temples in India also serve as pilgrimage centers. While the most popular deities like Shiva, Krishna, Vishnu, etc. all have many temples and murtis all around the world, some temples house one-of-a-kind deities. Madurai in South India is a city that is built around many grandiose Hindu temples, some of which are very unique. Devotees will often travel many miles several times a year to pay homage to their family deity. In Madurai, the marriage of the goddess Minakshi is not only a great festival but also a time when people may want to make the journey to see her. It is only proper that if the deity actually rests inside the murtis that believers attend the goddess' wedding.

Padmanabhaswamy Temple is dedicated to Vishnu

Early Vedic worship centered on fires, since fires were one of the most important elements in Vedic sacrifices. Back then, permanent structures for Hindu rituals were rare and location was not considered to be vital to the outcome or performance of the rite. However, location and image iconography eventually became extremely important. Some places, like the birthplace of Lord Rama in Ayodhya, would become pilgrimage spots simply because of their attested history. Other places gained temples simply because an auspicious recent event was seen to take place. Temples on the side of the road often emerged from natural formations, some as simple as an anthill. Often anthills became objects of worship because snakes, a key iconography element associated with the lord Shiva, would make their nests in the anthills. Therefore, a simple anthill could, over time, become a rather large temple site simply because the ants decided make their home there at that particular location.

Shaivites, devotees to the Lord Shiva, often build temples centered around lingams, a phallic symbol that represents Shiva. The erect phallus is surrounded by the round yoni, a symbol of the divine goddess's sexual power and organ. Vaishnavites, devotees to Vishnu, Krishna, and Rama, often worship the various manifestations of Vishnu. Alternatively, it is also popular for temples to contain images of scenes known from the literature, such as Vishnu resting on the cosmic serpent at the time of the creation of the world. Another popular scene is the goddess Kali stepping on Lord Shiva in the heat of a major battle.

Depiction of Kali

Art of this kind often invokes a particular type of emotion in the devotee. This emotion may lead to intense worship, perhaps the recitation of a mantra or piece of scripture, or maybe a donation to the temple if the devotee is so inclined. Alternatively, temples may also make money when their Brahmins are hired to perform rituals for patrons, such as marriage, or simply put the household deity to bed. In many villages, it is common for Brahmins to stop by individual private homes multiple times a day to tend to the deities housed therein.

People also need deities and Brahmins for other, simpler things. For instance, if a family wants to have a son, certain rituals may be performed. If a student needs assistance for an exam, a particular kind of blessing may be bestowed. The student may also pay homage to a particular deity, such as Sarasvati, who is associated with wisdom. Most deities have special powers and function as controllers of many elements in the natural world. The goddess Lakshmi, a consort of the god Vishnu, is always associated with wealth. However, in ancient times, she was also associated with kingship. Lakshmi's changing role in Hindu religious society is a testament to the ever fluid nature of Hindu religion.

Most pujas consist of offers of food, flowers, or incense. An arti is performed also, where a devotee waves a lighted lamp in front of the deity. Afterwards, people waft smoke from the fire over their head to gain the power or blessing from the deity. Many temples will also serve prasadam, which is food that has been offered and subsequently "eaten" and blessed by the deity. Consuming this food is a holy but delicious ritual for all.

As previously mentioned, in the Purusha Sukta portion of the Rg Veda, the cosmic man, Purusha, is divided into several parts: the head, the arms, the thighs, and the feet. Each symbolically represents the divisions of society. The Brahmins, or priests, are the head, the Kshatriyas, or kings and warriors, are the arms, the Vaishyas, or merchants, are the thighs, and the Shudras, or servents, are the feet. These four castes are called varnas, or "colors," in traditional Vedic society. It is unknown whether or not this caste system was intended to be prescriptive (i.e. how society should be arranged), or if it was merely descriptive (i.e. what the Vedic sages saw in their own society). Regardless, much has been written about the varna system and the type of societies it produces.

Elsewhere, classical Hindu literature describes the four major pursuits of people in a proper society. They are dharma (religion), artha (economics), kama (sense gratification), and moksha (liberation). It is only through the pursuit of these four aims that one can actually ever achieve a spiritual liberation. One needs material gain in order to embrace and enjoy the gratification of the senses, just as one needs sense pleasures to figure out that this temporary happiness is only fleeting and that moksha is the true aim of a person.

The four pursuits of man (purusha-artha) coincide with the prescribed stages of life. Often called the Ashrama system, a typical man should divide his life into carefully constructed stages, of which there are four. The first is being a brahmacharya (a student). Here a man leaves his family and studies at the Gurukula, a house with a renowned teacher. There the man acquires knowledge and learns how to live a righteous life.

Next, a man becomes a grhastha (householder). He takes a wife, has sons, gains wealth, and performs his duties to family and society admirably. Next, he retires (vanaprastha) and gradually becomes withdrawn from the world, instead dispensing wisdom during this stage. Finally, a man takes vows of renunciation (sannyasa) and becomes an ascetic, during which his entire being is devoted to seeking and achieving moksha, or release from birth and rebirth. Often sannyasins meditate until they die.

Despite many scriptures advocating this system, it is not a complete set of life situations for a man. In reality, most men do not lead a life that even remotely compares to this prescribed Ashrama system, and for every piece of scripture that advocates such a system, there is another piece that describes how ascetics are parasitic to society since they do not actively serve a productive role within society. However true this claim may or may not be, these same sorts of texts describe householders as the most honorable of men since they engage in dharma, kama, and artha simultaneously. One important facet of proper Vedic life involves offering the daily fire sacrifice, but even in medieval times the fire sacrifice could only be performed by householders. Therefore, full sannyasin renunciates are unable to perform some of the most vital rituals required of a person, according to the Vedas themselves. This philosophy fits in perfectly with the bhakti movements, such as the tradition described above begun by Chaitanya. To be a pure devotee of the lord, one does not need to renounce everything. As Lord Krishna says in the Bhagavad Gita, devotion is the highest and most efficient method to moksha, or liberation. Other types of yoga are viable, but perhaps not as easy.

The Prophecy

"Blessed is human birth, even the dwellers in heaven desire this birth, for true knowledge and pure love may be attained only by a human being." – attributed to Sri Krishna

Understanding Krishna as a deity requires fully understanding Vishnu, an integral part of the *Trimurti* – the holy trinity of creation and supreme divinity in Hinduism – alongside Brahma the Creator and Shiva the Destroyer, and the principal deity of Vaishnaism. Vishnu, otherwise known as "the Preserver," exudes unparalleled power, indubitable dominance, and effortless regality. The striking, four-armed god has a mesmerizing pair of heavy-lidded, almond-shaped eyes, blue skin ranging anywhere from light turquoise to a bold and electric, almost metallic cobalt-blue, and wore an elaborate golden headpiece decorated with a single peacock feather and studded with a rainbow of jewels atop his dark, flowing locks. Vishnu is typically seen with a bare, sculpted chest, partially covered by ornate necklaces and a *vaijayanti* (garland of forest flowers), and at times a shawl or a knee-length vest in a dazzling shade of butterscotch-yellow – the color of life, purity, knowledge, and peace – with a matching *dhoti*. His four arms are also ornamented with gold bangles and gem-encrusted wrist cuffs, and he wields a sacred object in each of his hands: a conch shell, a pink lotus flower, a gilded *gadā* (mace), and a *Sudarshana Chakra*, or the sun-shaped "discus of auspicious vision." The *vahana*, or "mounts" he is often depicted with, namely Sheshanaga, a thousand-headed serpent of seemingly endless length, and Garuda, a bird-like creature with the torso of a man and the head and great golden wings of an eagle, only enhance his splendor.

Neil Noland's picture of an ancient bust of Vishnu

Vishnu was given the momentous task of conserving the universe, maintaining order within the mortal realm, and protecting all its earthly inhabitants. While it was technically Brahma who designed the universe, Vishnu played an indispensable role – at least in the account of the Vishnu Purana – in the world's creation all the same. In the *Baghavata Purana*, it was also Vishnu who endowed all the other gods with the gift of immortality.

Before the mortal realm came to fruition, there was only Vishnu, curled up in deep slumber on the canopy of Sheshanaga's unfurled body, floating upon a cosmic ocean of milk. When he awoke, a lotus blossomed from his navel with the umbilical cord intact. Seated on the bed of this tremendous flower was a majestic being with four faces and arms named Brahma, who went on to map out and assemble the universe. The flower on which he was born was sectioned into three parts, forming the heavens, the sky, and the Earth. Brahma also had himself halved to create the first mortal man and woman. Plainly put, there would be no universe without Brahma, and no Brahma or Krishna without Vishnu.

Vishnu descended upon the mortal world time and time again to better protect mankind from evil and to restore order during turbulent times, each time taking on a different animal or human form. The first of the 10 incarnations or avatars of Vishnu, collectively known as the *Dashavatara*, was Matsya, a whale-sized gray fish who protected the ship of Shraddhadeva Manu from the roaring winds and upsurging, tempestuous waters of the Deluge. He returned to Earth a second time as Kurma, a gargantuan tortoise who retrieved a number of hallowed possessions that some of the gods had misplaced during the Deluge, and whose immense shell eventually formed the base of Mount Mandara. Vishnu's fifth avatar

Vamana, an unassuming, yet powerful dwarf, was conceived to put Mahabali, the cruel and covetous king of the Danavas, in his place. When the king agreed to grant Vamana ownership of any parcel of land that he could cover in three strides, the dwarf shape-shifted into a giant of staggering stature, his upper torso disappearing into the clouds, and proceeded to traverse over both heaven and earth in three earth-shaking steps, as promised.

This is the story of Vishnu's eighth avatar, Sri Krishna, also known as "Sanatanaya Namaha (The Eternal One)," "Sachidananda Vigrahaya Namaha (Embodiment of Existence, Awareness, and Bliss," and the "Yoginam Pataye Namaha (Lord of All Yogis)," among 105 other titles.

The parallels between Vishnu and Krishna are more bountiful and apparent in comparison to those between the former and the rest of his avatars.

Krishna, in many ways, was the spitting image of Vishnu, his breathtaking beauty perhaps one of, if not his most fabled attribute. Like Vishnu, Krishna had glossy, jet-black curls that cascaded down his back, paired with a slender, yet prominent nose and an entrancing gaze. He, too, is often portrayed with light sky-blue skin, but many believe his flesh had grayish undertones in the real world, as described by the *Brahma Samhita*: "[like that of] a new cloud...that does not correspond to any color in the material world...[and is] so beautiful that it surpasses the beauty of millions of cupids." In other accounts, Krishna's skin was a considerably richer and darker hue – a gorgeous blackish-blue shade reminiscent of the twilight sky. What's more, Krishna was also partial to bright canary-yellow ensembles and multicolored leis, and always garnished his hair, turban, or crown with an iridescent peacock feather.

Unlike Vishnu, however, Krishna was equipped with only two arms and was of average height – in some accounts, even below average – but could shrink or enlarge himself to any size he pleased, should the situation call for it. Moreover, the soles of Krishna's feet, his golden anklets jingling with every step, were marked with lotus flowers and auspicious chakra patterns. In *murti* representations, he is often seen playing a wooden or glittering gold flute said to be imbued with the power of seduction, for he was a sort of pied piper who attracted rambling lines of love-struck women and woodland critters alike. The flute is occasionally swapped out for a chakra disc or *gadā*, which were both bequeathed to him by the Vedic fire god, Agni.

Curiously enough, there are quite a few pieces of concrete evidence pointing to Krishna's existence. For starters, authors made it a point to chronicle his life, or at least reference him in numerous ancient Vedic texts such as the *Rig-Veda*, penned as early as 1500 BCE, the *Mahabharata,* and the *Bhagavata Purana,* the latter two authored in the first years of the Common Era. He was also depicted on primitive coins; Ananta Manikya, the ruler of the Tripura Kingdom in the 16th century BCE, issued silver Tankas, weighing roughly 10.72g, on which a flute-playing Krishna was featured, flanked by female attendants with flowers in hand.

In the late 1980s, a crew of archaeologists and expert divers captained by Dr. S. R. Rao from Goa's National Institute of Oceanography uncovered underwater structural remnants of what they believed to be Dwarka, supposedly founded by Krishna, just off the coast of present-day Dwarka in Gujarat. The same crew also unearthed two seals, which, according to the *Harivamsa,* were circulated by Krishna. Only those with said seal were permitted to enter his city.

While the aforementioned can be considered proof that Krishna was, in fact, a real individual who may very well have constructed and presided over the city of Dwarka, logically speaking, the tales of Krishna's supernatural powers and extravagant adventures were certainly embellished to a great extent. Furthermore, the anecdotes shared of Krishna's life, collectively referred to as the "Krishna Leela," were documented in reverse.

Krishna had always been an eminent protagonist in the lore of the Vrishni and Sattava tribes of the Yadava people, yet the popularization of the legendary figure in external circles only began in earnest in the 8th century BCE, around the same time he appeared in the *Chandogya Upanishad* – 2,000 to 2,500 years after Krishna's mortal death. These narratives, which painted Krishna – in addition to statesman and indomitable general – as a sage and preacher blessed with boundless wisdom, made no mention of Krishna's upbringing, arguably one of the most fascinating chapters of his life. In the 4th century BCE, Krishna was divinized in a grammar treatise entitled *"Ashtadhyayi,"* graduating from folk hero to full-fledged deity for the first time. It was then that Krishna became merged with Narayana-Vishnu – also two separate deities who had been previously been fused into one – by the Brahmins, and that the connection between Krishna and Vishnu was established. It was in the *Harivamsa,* composed in the 4th century CE, that the childhood component of his life was added to further flesh out his character. Certain elements of a god venerated by the cattle-tending Ahir people, who lived in settlements sprinkled throughout western and central India, were also incorporated into the fabled figure.

Skeptics may call attention to the glaring factual inconsistencies in the far-fetched details propagated about

Krishna's life, as well as the disorganization in the chronology of the Krishna narrative. Even so, an estimated 1.2 billion Hindus and devout yogis continue to pay homage to this one-of-a-kind divinity without reservation. Some adherents insist that those who provided these otherworldly descriptions of Krishna were in no way delusional, and had instead been granted the privilege of seeing him in his most authentic form as a reward for their devotion. Some acknowledge the quixotic and unrealistic aspects of both Krishna's story and the leading man himself, but choose to view the former as a collection of allegorical tales abounding in morals centered on a real-life manifestation of Vishnu, who, while not necessarily a magical being per se, was a philosopher and sacred guru that should be revered all the same.

To Krishna's disciples, he was unlike any other god. He was the quintessential child prodigy, a lovable prankster, an irresistible heartthrob, the personification of pure romance, an honorable statesman, a divine protector, a spiritual leader, a faithful friend, and the universal supreme being rolled into one. Of course, in order to gain a better understanding of the glorification of Krishna, one must first journey through the spellbinding saga of his life in the mortal world.

5,000 years ago, the Kingdom of Mathura in Uttar Pradesh was governed by a gracious and magnanimous king named Ugrasena. Ugrasena had two children – a son named Kamsa (also spelled "Kansa") and a daughter, Devaki, with his consort, Queen Padmavati. Like her father, the ravishing Devaki was a gentle soul. Kamsa, on the other hand, was an irredeemably evil and wretchedly oppressive tyrant, in some accounts said to be a demon in disguise.

When Kamsa came of age, the power-hungry prince forcibly dethroned his aging father and dragged the now-former monarch to the palace dungeon. Kamsa's subjects were miserable under the crushing weight of Kamsa's iron fist. The self-professed king was a war-mongering brute who joined forces with Jarasandha, the cruel king of Magadha, and often attacked the neighboring kingdom of the Yadu tribe unprovoked, taxed and stole from his subjects, and imprisoned anyone who dared to question his authority. The citizens of Mathura were desperate to free themselves of Kamsa's despotic regime and prayed for salvation. Brahma heeded their heartfelt pleas and sought the aid of Vishnu to end the people's suffering. Vishnu vowed to return to Earth to liberate not only Mathura, but also the downtrodden subjects of neighboring kingdoms from Kamsa and other fascistic kings.

After deliberating with his advisers, Kamsa yielded his blessings to Devaki, who wished to marry Vasudeva, the prince and later king of the Yadava tribe. His sister's happiness had nothing to do with his decision; instead, he assumed that the marriage automatically entitled him to all the lands within the Yadava domain. Kamsa was so keen on the prospect of absorbing the Yadava territories into his kingdom that he financed and attended the wedding – a grand affair complete with a sumptuous feast, live music, lavish costumes, and thousands upon thousands of guests.

Following the celebrations, Kamsa personally escorted the newlyweds to their new palace via the royal carriage. Kamsa and the lovebirds were just minutes away from their destination when a thundering voice suddenly boomed from above. The chariot jerked off course for a moment before screeching to a halt.

"Kamsa," the disembodied voice from the heavens addressed him directly. "Now that your sister is married to the Yadava prince, know that your days on earth are numbered. The eighth son of Devaki and Vasudeva shall end your tyrannical rule in Mathura and kill you."

In another less-theatrical version of this story, the revelation was brought about by a fortune teller whom Kamsa had consulted shortly after the wedding.

Either way, Kamsa was both deeply shaken by this divine prophecy that foretold his inevitable doom. He unsheathed his sword and raised it above his head with an unhinged look in his eyes and prepared to plunge the blade into his sister's stomach. After all, without Devaki, there would be no slayer.

Kamsa would have dispatched or irreversibly mutilated the womb of his own flesh and blood had it not been for Vasudeva, who dropped to his knees and implored his brother-in-law to spare his wife. Vasudeva pledged to surrender each and every one of his children upon their births and allowed the merciless king to do with them as he wished. Kamsa narrowed his eyes in thought for a few moments before finally lowering his sword. Vasudeva's word alone, however, was not enough. To preclude Devaki and Vasudeva from flaking on their promise and fleeing, or swapping out their eighth newborn for one unrelated to them and presenting him as their own, he tossed them into a squalid cell in a nearby prison, where their every move would be observed by eagle-eyed guards.

Although the prophesy explicitly identified Devaki and Vasudeva's eighth son as Kamsa's assassin, the paranoid potentate refused to take any chances. Kamsa prized his nieces and nephews from the arms of his inconsolable sister and remorseful brother-in-law six times in a row, and flung them against the wall, bashing their heads in and killing them instantly. The seventh son of Devaki and Vasudeva, however, was spared from this atrocity. As soon as their seventh son, who came to be known as "Balarama," was conceived, Vishnu removed the embryo from Devaki's womb and planted it in the belly of Rohini, Vasudeva's first wife. The stillborn child that Devaki produced was no more than an empty vessel. Balarama, born on the Shravan Purnima, the full moon of the fifth Hindu month, and in some accounts the second incarnation of Sheshanaga, would also become a god in his own right.

Needless to say, Devaki, Vasudeva, and Kamsa were equally troubled by the news of Devaki's eighth pregnancy, albeit for radically different reasons.

At last, the prophetic day came. It was the eve of the *Ashtami*, or the eighth day of Shravan – estimated to be July 19th or 20th sometime between 3228 and 3112 BCE. It soon became abundantly apparent that this would be no ordinary day. The brilliant turquoise skies had been perfectly clear throughout daytime, but come nightfall, the fluffy, placid clouds started to swirl and heave. Avalanches of torrential rainfall surged down from the skies, accompanied by howling gales that threatened to rip entire houses from their foundations. The normally tranquil waters of the holy Yamuna River swelled and pulsed, its embankments bursting in a matter of minutes.

The plump baby boy, who remained nameless for the time being, was born at the stroke of midnight. There was no physical act of childbirth; rather, the boy vanished from Devaki's womb, who slept like a log through the whole process, and miraculously appeared in the cradle next to her. Once the boy materialized, a blinding ray of light radiated from the crib, illuminating every inch of the somber prison cell. Devaki, who did not even flinch, remained sound asleep, but Vasudeva was jolted awake at once.

The boy was born with four hands, but Vasudeva, upon seeing this, furiously prayed for the gods to remove his extra limbs, so as to "conceal his divinity." Vasudeva's prayers were answered in mere seconds, and he watched in rapt astonishment as the cooing infant retracted the excess arms back into his body. In most accounts, the boy's stunning dark skin was a deep lapis-blue hue from the moment of his birth. In other accounts, there was nothing unusual about the shade of his dark complexion for the first year or so of his life. The boy was then given a poisoned drink (or a piece of tainted fruit) which, of course, had no effect on him, but stained his skin blue.

Vasudeva was rocking the boy back and forth in his arms in the corner of the cell, ineffectively cloaking the light emanating from the infant whilst keeping an ear out for the eerily silent guards when the same silvery voice reverberated from above, drowning out the sounds of the raging storm.

"On your feet, Vasudeva," commanded the voice. "This is your newborn son. Take him to Gokul, where your friend Nandraj (the head of the Gopa tribe) lives, and leave him in his house. His wife, Yashoda, has also borne a daughter tonight, but they are unaware of her birth. Leave your son with them and return to this cell with their daughter. Nandraj and Yashoda will never know of the exchange and will raise your son as their own."

The bright light was extinguished as quickly as it came. Now, Vasudeva's battered heart cracked in two yet again at the thought of parting with yet another child, but he pushed himself to focus on the task at hand. As he was emptying out a wicker basket just large enough to hold the precious cargo, the rusty iron gate of his cell swung open of its own accord. He then balanced the basket on his head, which he had covered with a square of cloth, and crept past the guards, who had all slumped down to the floor – the result of a temporary sleeping spell – and out of the prison.

Vasudeva headed towards the seething Yamuna river. His heart sank to his stomach upon spotting the cemetery of broken boats. Nevertheless, he soldiered on, powering through with his unwavering faith in the gods, and entered the river on foot. Much to his relief, the river calmed and magically subsided with every step he took. Moments later, Sheshanaga himself emerged and hovered over Vasudeva and his basket with its cluster of heads, essentially serving as a roof and shielding them from the wind and rain.

Vasudeva slipped into the home of Nandraj (or Nanda Maharaja) and Yashoda, and snuck into the bedchamber unnoticed. There, he found the baby girl stirring next to the snoozing couple and quietly made the trade. Like Devaki, Yashoda, who knew not the sex of her child, would not realize that she had skipped the act of childbirth until her awakening. The tearful Vasudeva kissed his son goodbye, and with the baby girl in his arms, trekked back to the prison.

The baby girl started bawling the moment she was set down in the unfamiliar cradle. Devaki, the guards, and Kamsa, who was sleeping on the floor above their cell in anticipation of his nephew's birth, simultaneously awoke with a start. Devaki, groggy and confused, reached for the baby instinctively, and Vasudeva, who was pretending to rub the sleep from his eyes, pointed out the baby's gender.

Kamsa shoved past the guards, berating them for failing to notify him about the birth sooner, and barged into their cell. Devaki showed Kamsa the telling lack of an appendage between the baby's legs and pleaded with her brother to reconsider. She had borne a girl, Devaki reasoned, which meant that the prophecy was false.

Alas, Devaki's pleas fell on deaf ears. Kamsa overpowered Devaki and lobbed the infant against the wall. Vasudeva pulled Devaki to his chest and covered her ears, but that sickening splat never came. To the bewilderment of all those present, the baby floated in mid-air and transformed into Durga, the eight-armed goddess of strength, mounted upon a lion and brandishing a different weapon in each fist.

"Kamsa," Durga bellowed. "Your slayer has already been born, and he is alive and well. One day, he will hunt you down, punish you, and kill you for all the evils you've done. From this day forward, you will find no peace, and will be haunted by the thoughts of your inevitable demise."

And with that, Durga disappeared.

The frightening encounter with the goddess, the reality of which was solidified by two other witnesses, left Kamsa shell-shocked. He barely slept a wink and lost his appetite for several days. But rather than reflect on his behavior and attempt to change his ways, his untameable arrogance – he had somehow credited himself with preventing the birth of his assassin in his prison– led him to convince himself that he could still alter his fate.

How wrong he was.

Youth & Adolescence

"Do everything you have to do, but not with ego, not with lust, not with envy, but with love, compassion, humility, and devotion." – attributed to Sri Krishna

The villagers of Gokul were utterly enraptured by the blue-skinned newborn – the unprecedented product of a divine birth. They flocked to the residence of Nandraj and Yashoda in droves, queuing up to offer blessings and gifts of fruit baskets, pearls, and an assortment of other trinkets. There was something remarkably special about this baby boy, though they could not quite put their finger on it. Apart from his stupendous beauty, they marveled at his invariably cheerful and effervescent disposition. The boy, who had an electrifying twinkle in his eyes, never cried or fussed, and always greeted his visitors with a radiantly sunny smile – one that instilled joy, hope, and an inexplicable sense of calm to those who received it.

Other children were equally captivated by the child, who came round to Nandraj and Yashoda's home day in and day out to play with him. This affection was always reciprocated, but his favorite playmate was Nandraj's fair-skinned nephew, Balarama – neither boy had yet been assigned a name at this point – who moved in with his mother (and Nandraj's cousin) Rohini shortly after his birth to escape Kamsa's tyranny. It is important to note that while Rohini and the foster parents knew that Balarama was the son of Vasudeva, they were unaware that the souls of Krishna and Balarama had originated in Devaki's womb, and that they were, in reality, brothers, which explained the natural bond between them.

It was impossible to imagine that anyone would have the heart – or rather, lack of – to hurt this sweet, innocent child, and yet, this was precisely the case. A dark, menacing cloud loomed over the newborn, no more than a few days old, in the form of his uncle Kamsa, who was resolved to snuff out his existence at any cost. The elimination of the child, Kamsa believed, was the only way to nullify the prophecy.

About a week later, Kamsa traveled to the gloomy peripheries of the woodlands in the fringes of his kingdom, and hiked up to a cold, shadowy cave inhabited by a *multo* (ghost) named Putana. The demoness was a tall, hideous beast with greasy, scraggly hair, bulging, soulless eyes, blackened tusks, yellowed, curling nails, and reeked of rotting eggs. As the child's whereabouts were unknown, Putana was tasked with tracking down and killing all the children in his kingdom born in the last 10 days. The *multo*, who sought any opportunity to terrorize mortals, readily accepted the mission.

Putana rolled up her proverbial sleeves and went to work at once. Disguising herself as an attractive young maiden and adopting a meek demeanor to evade suspicion, she spent the next few days hunting down all the newborns in Kamsa's realm, as well as those in neighboring kingdoms for good measure. She slunk into the homes of new parents after sundown and waited until they fell asleep, busied themselves with chores, or were otherwise distracted, before snatching up their infants.

Eventually, Putana arrived in Gokul. The contagious excitement of the villagers, who were endlessly gushing over the newborn of a woman named Yashoda, signified that she had come to the right place. She retreated into the shadows and waited for the following morning to make her move.

Come dawn, Putana snared the most poisonous snake she could find and smeared its venom all over her nipples. She then returned to Gokul and joined the visitors filing into Yashoda's residence. Putana introduced herself to Yashoda and requested permission to nurse her son. Struck by Putana's false beauty, Yashoda assumed that the stranger was a goddess descended from the heavens to sanctify her son, and gladly handed him over to her.

Putana carried the newborn to the backyard and allowed him to latch onto her. And latch on he did. Rather than go into shock, the boy suckled with more and more vigor, draining the life out of the *multo*. Putana screeched and tried to detach the baby from her teat, to no avail. She then shifted back to her true form in an attempt to frighten the child, and still, the boy clung on. Hearing this ruckus, Yashoda and the other guests hastened to the backyard, only to find the giggling baby seated on the ground, completely unharmed. Sprawled out next to him, however, was the shriveled and lifeless body of Putana.

The foster parents knew that the boy was special, but his true capabilities surpassed all expectations. The boy was more than merely a bewitchingly beautiful child with a magnetic personality. He was a sacred being equipped with unfathomable powers – the likes of which no one had ever seen. And yet, this was only a glimpse of what was to come.

In some accounts, the child's foster parents appealed to their *Kulguru* (family priest), Garga (Sage) Muni, directly to name their child, along with Rohini's son. In other accounts, it was Vasudeva who employed Garga Muni, in this version a trusted high-ranking priest of the Yadu tribe, to name and calculate the Vedic horoscope of his sons. And so, as instructed by Vasudeva, Muni journeyed to Gokul under the guise of conducting other business, and visited the home of Nandraj and Yashoda.

Nandraj, who answered the door, was pleasantly surprised by the arrival of the unexpected visitor, and welcomed him with open arms. He was well-acquainted with the garga's glowing reputation, who, on top of being well-versed in the Vedas and Puranas, had authored a number of impressive astrological texts, including the *Garga Samhita*. Muni made no mention of Vasudeva, as per his word. Instead, he explained that he had heard all about the boy wonder from the other villagers, and felt compelled to perform the *Namkaran* (naming ceremony) for and offer his blessings to the newborns of the house.

Namkaran were typically celebrated with great pageantry, but with Kamsa and his infernal henchmen prowling around the kingdom in search of the prophetic child, Muni chose to hold a discreet ceremony in the couple's cattle shed. The name of Rohini's one-year-old son, given his seniority, was determined first. Rohini, said Muni, was born to be a leader, having been given the sacred gift of dispensing wisdom, justice, and transcendental bliss to all those around him. For this, he received one part of his name: "Rama," named after Lord Rama, Vishnu's seventh avatar. Strength and valiance were also in his cards, earning him the second part of his name: "Bala." Thus, he was thenceforth known as "Balarama."

The blue-skinned tot was also destined for greatness, but on a significantly more extraordinary scale. This boy was to become the greatest of and friend to all cowherds and bovines, and would bring good fortune and drastic, lasting change. Legions of murderous demons, Muni cautioned, would target the child on multiple occasions, but his foster parents could rest assured that he would be protected by the almighty Vishnu himself. Muni assigned to him the name "Krishna," meaning "waning fortnight" or "dark and all-attractive," after slipping into and awakening from a meditative trance – a reference to the boy's unique complexion.

Much to the dismay of Krishna's foster parents, Muni's predictions regarding the demonic hitmen proved true.

Fast forward to Krishna's first birthday. In the midst of the festivities, Yashoda noticed Krishna yawning, and decided to place him onto a cushion underneath a *sakata* (household cart), where he could nap in peace. Little did she know that the *sakata* next to his was Shakatasur, a *multo* that had transformed himself into a trolley, hiding in plain sight and lying in wait for the opportunity to strike.

Krishna's intuition served him well. Sensing something amiss, the infant began to wail for his mother, but his cries were muffled by the party's vibrant music and loud chatter. Upon observing this, Shakatasur returned to his real form, climbed on top of the *sakata*, and began pushing down with all his weight in a bid to crush the child.

Krishna did not panic. Rather, he began to titter and kicked at the cart's wheel repeatedly with his tiny lotus feet, believing this to be a game of some sort. Suddenly, the *sakata* rocketed into the air and fell back down to earth with such force that the cart and all its contents – brass dishes and jugs of milk, butter, and curd – splintered into hundreds of pieces, as if it had been mowed over by a much larger vehicle. The adults, hearing this resounding clang, rushed over to inspect the commotion with their hearts in their throats. Their reaction was once more a mixture of relief and incredulity. Krishna was casually lapping the milk that had spilled from one of the shattered vessels. Behind him was a dead demon, trapped underneath the remnants of the *sakata*.

Kamsa, who received word of Shakatasur's demise shortly thereafter, was furious, but undeterred, and enlisted the aid of an even more powerful demon.

A few days later, Krishna wandered out to the courtyard as Yashoda was preparing supper. Krishna was playing with some furry critters who had made their home in one of their trees when a demon named Trinavarta, who took the shape of a tornado, came and whisked the child away. As Trinavarta spiraled upwards into the clouds, a dense and impenetrable billow of dust and dirt blanketed every inch of Gokul. Yashoda sprinted to the courtyard, sobbing and shrieking as she groped around for her missing baby, but Krishna, oblivious to the danger, clapped and cheered as if he were on some carnival ride.

Trinavarta, who was carrying Krishna on his shoulders, was preparing to drop the child from a great height. When Krishna cottoned on to this, he firmed himself on the demon's shoulders, and enlarged his body, and in turn, his weight. Trinavarta began to wobble from side to side, struggling to support the rapidly growing burden, and was left with no choice but to lower himself back to earth. In the midst of the descent, Krishna, who had expanded to the size of a mountain, seized the demon by the neck. The gurgling Trinavarta tried to wriggle free from Krishna's grasp, but the infant's grip was so strong that his eyes popped out of their sockets. When Trinavarta fell still, Krishna dropped the demon and cushioned his own fall with its corpse.

Not long after Krishna's third birthday, Nandraj and Yosheda packed their belongings, loaded their infants into a *sakata*, and headed for Vrindavan, situated 11.2 miles north of Gokul, in the hopes of shaking the demons off Krishna's trail. The move, while well-intentioned, however, did nothing to keep these demons at bay.

The first of these demons to sniff out Krishna's scent was Bakasur, an enormous, ghastly black crane with a gigantic, blood-stained beak and razor-sharp talons. Krishna and Balarama were monkeying around with their friends in a nearby forest one afternoon when the avian demon spotted its target. A piercing squawk filled the air, and in the next instant, Bakasur swooped down, clamped its beak around Krishna's body, and swallowed him whole.

Krishna's chums dispersed in all directions, blubbering as they called for help. Of course, the hysteria, though understandable, was unnecessary. The children simmered down as soon as Bakasura started retching and flapping his wings erratically, and plummeted back down to earth with a loud thud. Krishna came hurtling out of the bird's beak in a jet of flames, and tumbled onto the grass. He then stepped onto Bakasura's lower mandible, grabbed hold of its upper beak, and tore the bird cleanly in half as if ripping a sheet of paper.

A few years later, Kamsa learned that Krishna, now five or six, was being schooled in cattle herding, and planned the next hit accordingly.

After locating a dewy patch of grass for their charges one morning, Krishna and Balarama plopped themselves down on a river bank and dug into their lunch, all the while keeping an eye on their calves. They then whipped out their flutes, hoping to squeeze in a brief jam session, only to be interrupted by the whimpering of their calves.

Balarama was baffled by the sudden skittishness of the cows, the young bovines inching away from one of the calves. Krishna cocked his head to one side and pointed at the strange animal, which, at first glance, appeared to be no different than any of the other cows. "That is not one of ours," revealed Krishna. "That is a demon posing as a cow, and it has come to kill me."

Krishna was right. The seemingly gentle calf was indeed a demon named Vatsasura, another one of Kamsa's *multo* minions. Before Balarama could assess this information, his brother pounced on the demon calf, wrapped his fingers around its tail and hind leg, and whirled it around like a hammer thrower before releasing his hold. The calf was sent flying into a tree, the blow snapping its neck and every one of its limbs, and was dead before it hit the ground.

Now, even with Krishna's flawless record, the demons just kept on coming. A serpent fiend named Aghasura, perhaps having taken notes of its predecessors' failures, opted for a more creative approach.

At the crack of dawn one morning, Krishna climbed up a nearby hill and sounded his buffalo horn, summoning hundreds of his cow-herding friends to their usual spot in the woods for a picnic and some playtime. Some of the boys brushed their cows' coats. Some dressed up with flower garlands and peacock feathers in their hair, daubed their cheeks with red and yellow clay, and engaged in pretend play. Others kicked and tossed *amalaki* (Indian gooseberry) and *bael* (golden apple) fruits, which they used as balls. Two of the boys were eventually made to enter a thicket to retrieve one of the *bael* balls.

Moments later came the pitter-pattering of small, running feet. The breathless boys poked their heads of the thicket, hardly able to contain their enthusiasm. "Boys!" the pair exclaimed, gesturing wildly. "Come with us, and hurry!"

Intrigued, Krishna and the rest of the boys followed the pair and cut through the grove, soon after reaching another clearing. Jaws dropped all around as they beheld what appeared to be a colossal, tunnel-like cave that stretched on for miles and miles. Only Krishna could see the cave for what it truly was. It was no cave at all, but rather, the cavernous mouth of Aghasura, an 8-mile-long black python. The fact that the serpent demon was the younger brother of Putana and Bakasura was no coincidence; he was here to exact vengeance for the deaths of his siblings.

Krishna warned his friends to stay back, but the boys, who could not peel their eyes away from the seductive golden glow within the cave, ignored him, marching right into the serpent's mouth and straight into its belly. Krishna, presumably shaking his head in disappointment, chased after them. Predictably, as soon as Krishna entered Aghasura's mouth, the python locked its jaws. Terrified, the boys clawed at the walls of the "cave" and shouted for their mothers.

Krishna hushed the boys and urged them to keep a cool head. There was nothing to be afraid of, he consoled them, for he had a plan. The boys watched in amazement as Krishna assumed his position in the middle of the cave, his arms and legs splayed, and proceeded to swell in size. He grew larger and larger, sinking his nails into the fleshy walls, until Aghasura's airway was wholly obstructed. The boys rolled around like dice in a dome as Aghasura thrashed around violently, gasping for air, and they, too, fell unconscious. When the python finally expired, Krishna carried each and every one of the boys out of the

serpent's slackened jaw and roused them with his
"transcendental glance."

The gods observed Krishna's every move from above
and were profoundly impressed with the boy's talents.
Brahma, on the contrary, was secretly envious and
outwardly skeptical of Krishna's abilities, and decided to
put them to the test. The challenge would not involve any
demons – the boy had already more than proven himself
as a fearless warrior – and instead, would be a test of his
ingenuity and the depth of his powers.

Like most other afternoons, Krishna and his fellow cow-
herders were posted up next to a grazing meadow and
crystal-clear lake. The boys snacked on fruits freshly
picked from their surrounding trees and began to clown
around for some time, as children are wont to do. They
were so invested in their tomfoolery that they downright
forgot to check in on their flock.

"Oh, no!" cried one of the boys. "Our cows!"

Krishna and the cow-herders swung around in unison.
Their cows had roamed so far away from the grazing
point that they had been reduced to specks in the distance.
Krishna, the elected leader of the boys, felt an immediate
pang of shame for neglecting his responsibilities, and
volunteered to fetch the cows. It was then that Brahma
took action. With Krishna gone, he transported all the

boys and calves to a magical, secluded cave in a supernatural realm.

Krishna searched high and low for the lost cows, but unable to locate them, made his way back to the boys with his tail between his legs. Unfortunately, they, too, were long gone. His despair was further compounded the next day when he learned that none of the boys had returned home the previous evening, who had, as a group, apparently dematerialized into thin air.

Nothing could prepare Brahma for what awaited him when he returned to the mortal realm a week (in some accounts, a full year) later. He was, in a word, floored. It appeared that Krishna had multiplied himself into the exact number of boys and calves that had "mysteriously" disappeared. To be clear, they were not replicas of Krishna, but instead, the carbon copies of each and every one of the missing boys. The detail of Krishna's work was exquisite; each duplicate shared the same hairstyle, distinctive facial features, precise birthmarks, and unique personality quirks with his original, and was even sporting the same clothes and satchel – packed with identical contents – that they were last seen in. The same applied to the bovine doubles, each animal bearing the same spots as their respective counterparts.

Brahma was humbled. It was then that it dawned on him. He was merely the creator of one universe; Krishna, through Vishnu, was the "original creator of infinite universes." When he returned all the original cow-herders and their flock, their duplicates faded out of sight. Never again would Brahma – or any other god, for that matter – question Krishna's powers.

Krishna was undoubtedly a gifted child, to say the least, but he was also, in many ways, like any other average youngster.

He was, for instance, a merry prankster at heart. Krishna and his friends often shimmied down into people's houses through loose tiles on their roof. They had no interest in any of the jewelry or valuables laying around the house. The sweet-tooths had only one item on their agenda: butter. They clambered onto each other's shoulders, forming a human ladder, to the pots of butter and buttermilk on the topmost shelves, which were specifically stored at these great heights to keep them out of children's reach. If this failed, the butter burglars pelted the jars with stones until they cracked, and caught the dribbles of buttermilk with their open mouths below.

The growing boy, like most other lads his age, also began to develop an interest in girls, but the attention that he received from the opposite sex was, to put it mildly, beyond compare. He was, supposedly without exaggeration, the object of all the village girls' desires. There wasn't a single girl who did not blush and giggle uncontrollably in his presence, and who did not compete for his time and affection.

Gopis, or unmarried cow-herding girls between the ages of 10 and 14, regularly congregated at his favorite haunt – a quiet glade near his home with magnificent acoustics – every sunset without fail. There, they danced with great animation to the exuberant tunes that Krishna played from his flute. This dance, called the "Rasa Leela," which translates to "play of aesthetics," is alternatively known as the "Dance of Divine Love." Sometimes, Krishna, a master storyteller, entertained them with riveting tales of adventure and romance, and the gopis hung on to his every word for hours on end. When Krishna was not in the mood to do either of these things, the girls joined him in his idleness, staring into space in complete silence and simply savoring his company.

The gopis, who yearned for nothing other than Krishna's hand in marriage, performed the *Agrahayana* religiously in the autumn month of *Hemanta* (October-November) every year. The *Agrahayana*, a love ritual that revolved around the goddess Durga, AKA "Katayani," promised a loving husband to all those who paid adequate tribute to the deity. The rite was a rather complex process.

Every morning, the gopis prepared *havisyanna* – a soupy, turmeric-free and spice-less meal made out of boiled rice and moong dal that was meant to "purify" their bodies. Afterwards, they took a dip in the sacred Yamuna River to further cleanse their bodies and souls. The daily worship itself mainly consisted of fashioning a doll out of sand, earth, and minerals (for pigment) taken from the riverbank; others sculpted their dolls out of wood or stone, which were then painted and adorned with jewels and other accessories. These dolls were then presented to Durga on an ornate altar decorated with incense lamps, floral wreaths, and offerings of fruits and grains.

All this was done in the name of Krishna. And yet, even with the throngs of comely and eligible young women pining after him day by day, Krishna's heart, they say, only belonged to one.

Like many of the greatest romances, Krishna's first encounter with whom many call the love of his life, was the fruit of sweet serendipity.

After churning a pot of buttermilk on the stove one lazy afternoon, Yashoda ducked out of the kitchen for a bit to run a quick errand. Catching a whiff of the fresh, bubbling butter in the air, the insatiable Krishna tiptoed into the kitchen and attempted to sneak a few slurps on the sly. His gluttony and impatience, however, would cost him.

When Krishna dunked his fingers into the scalding-hot butter, he jerked backwards with a loud yelp and caused the entire vessel to topple over. Sweeping the shards away into one corner, the boy dropped to his hands and knees and guzzled up as much of the spilled buttermilk as he could. Unable to finish the buttermilk on his own, Krishna whistled at a troop of monkeys perched on a nearby tree and invited them in to assist him with the damage control.

Krishna and the monkeys, who failed to hear the approaching footsteps, were caught red-handed. Flustered, Yashoda shooed the monkeys out of her kitchen and hauled the mischievous boy into the backyard by the ear. After dishing out an earful, she bound Krishna's waist to a hefty grindstone to teach him a lesson once and for all.

There, Krishna remained tethered to the grindstone for quite some time, pondering the consequences of his butter heists. Naturally, he soon became restless, and feeling the itch to stretch his legs, sprung to his feet. Moving the slab of rock normally required the strength of at least two grown men, but to Krishna, the grindstone was practically weightless.

The troublemaker sauntered into the woods with the grindstone in tow. To his annoyance, the wheel became wedged between a pair of trees. With just one sharp tug, the trees came crashing down to the ground, and in the process, Krishna inadvertently liberated the souls of Kubera's sons, who had been transformed into said trees via a curse inflicted by Garga Narada.

Krishna proceeded to rove around aimlessly until he stumbled upon a jagged boulder, which he used to saw through the rope. Slick with sweat from all the physical exertion and the sweltering summer heat, he flopped down next to a berry bush and fished out his flute. Just then, two young maidens who were passing through strayed from their paths and floated his way, drawn to the hypnotic melody wafting through the woods.

Krishna recognized the younger of the pair – a neighbor girl named Laliltha who often came round for supper and celebratory gatherings. He was, however, much too captivated by the intoxicating beauty of her companion to pay her any mind. Only when he finally managed to collect his scattered thoughts did he muster up the courage to inquire her name. Her name, she said, was Radha Rani, the daughter of Vrishabhanu Maharaj, a modest cow-herder who hailed from the village of Barsana. The attraction was mutual, and she, too, fell victim to love at first sight. "I knew from then on, that I would live in him," Radha would later say. "And that he would live in me. It does not matter where he is or who he is with, for he will always remain in my heart."

Although Krishna had never met Radha prior to this encounter, it occurred to him, after a few moments of gazing into her expressive, chocolate-brown eyes, that he knew precisely who she was – or rather, who she used to be. She was the incarnation of Shakti, his one true love from a previous lifetime. From that day forward, the young lovebirds spent almost every waking moment together, and were so inseparable that they are now often thought to be a single, unified being, aptly dubbed "Radha Krishna," which represents the melding of the masculine and feminine "realities" of God.

In the meantime, Krishna continued to exterminate the swarms of demons that continued to harass him and the Vrindavan villagers. One such beast was a rabid bull demon named Arishtasura, who knocked down dozens of trees, mangled a season's worth of crops, demolished multiple houses beyond repair, and trampled several of the livestock to death, among other forms of mayhem. Upon taking stock of the carnage, Krishna flew into a fit of rage and charged at the bull head on, breaking Arishtasura's neck and shattering his horns in one fell swoop.

Garga Narada, who witnessed Krishna's superhuman strength firsthand, traveled to Mathura and informed Kamsa of the incident. There was no need to look any further, Narada proclaimed, for he was certain with every fiber of his being that Krishna, son of Nandraj and

Yosheda, was the eighth-born son of Devaki and Vasudeva. And with that, Kamsa and Narada hatched a new plan.

Justice

"Among weapons I am the thunderbolt, among cows I am the wish-fulfilling cow called 'Surabhi,' among serpents I am Vasuki, I am the progenitor, the god of Love." – attributed to Sri Krishna

While Radha and Krishna are now often regarded as a single entity, two souls eternally intertwined as one, they were, in reality, the definition of star-crossed lovers. Their paths diverged when Arthura, Kamsa's servant, invited Krishna and Balarama to Mathura. King Kamsa, Arthura explained, had caught wind of the thrilling tales regarding the brothers' stupendous strength and all their phenomenal feats, and was anxious to meet them in person. They would be the guest of honors in the sacred Festival of the Bow – a glorious celebration dedicated to Lord Shiva – and had been gifted the great privilege of competing in the main event: a traditional wrestling match called *"Bahuyuddha."*

The day before their departure, the sweethearts rendezvoused at the place of their first meeting. As they clung on to one another, Radha pledged her heart to him, and vowed to wait for him always, even if it took hundreds, or even thousands of years. Sadly, Radha was unable to deliver on her promise, though through no fault of her own. Just weeks after Krishna left for Vrindavan, her domineering mother coerced her into marrying another man by the name of Vaishya Rayan, who, according to some accounts, was Krishna's adoptive maternal uncle. Excluding a pretend wedding that took place towards the latter years of their adolescence, Krishna and Radha were never legally married.

Meanwhile, Kamsa, who had been tipped off to Vasudeva's central role in the late-night baby-swap, and once again arrested both Vasudeva and Devaki to punish them for their deception.

Once they were back in the dungeons, Kamsa dusted off his hands and continued to lay the spadework for the arrival of the legendary brothers. In the days leading up to the festival, Kamsa marshaled together the burliest, fiercest, and most highly-trained wrestlers in all of Mathura. He hand-picked Chanura for the first round, pitting him against Krishna, and selected Mushtika as Balarama's opponent. Chanura and Mushtika were easily the most intimidating in Kamsa's elite wrestling team. Chanura was a particularly oafish, yet vicious mountain of a man, who was infamous for preying on the old and infirm, and raping helpless young women.

On the day of the wrestling match, thousands of spectators poured into the royal *akharas* (an ancient outdoor stadium) to behold the grand event. The atmosphere, marked by adrenaline-charged suspense and intense, but good-natured competitive spirits took a drastic turn as soon as Krishna and Balarama's contenders stepped into the ring. The audience took offense to the egregious age difference and disproportionate disparity in the weight classes between the two teams. Krishna and Balarama, 16 and 17 respectively, were amateur wrestlers, whereas seasoned professionals Chanura and Mushtika were well into middle age, and were twice the size of the brothers.

The jeering spectators called for Kamsa to either cancel the matches altogether or to replace his starters, but Krishna and Balarama held up their hands and silenced the crowd. They had already accepted Kamsa's terms, and would therefore do the honorable thing and proceed with the match as planned. Kamsa scoffed at what he perceived to be the brothers' arrogance, and leaned forward in his seat, clasping his hands in anticipation. Now that he had lured Krishna to Mathura, he had the blue-skinned nuisance in the palm of his hand and would be rid of him in no time; after all, he had the home-court advantage.

To the audience's amazement and Kamsa's confusion – quickly followed by blazing fury – both Krishna and

Balarama emerged victorious in the first two rounds, and had not a single scratch on their bodies. Their opponents, while only lightly wounded, were forced to cope with their severely bruised egos. Humiliated, Chanura decided to resort to dirty tricks for the third round, openly flouting the cardinal rule of *Bahuyuddha*, which strictly forbade the deliberate murder of one's opponent.

Chanura busted out his trademark move; he shoved Krishna and pinned him to the ground, so as to crush him, but the latter simply rolled out from underneath him and sprung back to his feet. The growling Chanura swung at Krishna's head vigorously, but the nimble-footed teenager daintily hopped from side to side, almost as if he were dancing, and dodged every blow. Krishna, aware of Chanura's intentions, decided to beat him to the punch. He seized Chanura by the hand and spun him around dozens of times before releasing him. When Chanura finally fell back down to earth, he had been reduced to a fleshy sack of broken ribs and bones. Moments later, Balarama knocked Mushtika off his feet with a swipe of his leg, whereupon he clobbered him to death with his deceptively powerful fists.

Several other wrestlers waiting in the wings took their turns, but they, too, were finished off in similar fashion. The remaining wrestlers, petrified by the lifeless bodies littered across the ring, threw in their towels without ever setting foot into the ring. The raucous applause that rang through the arena was deafening.

Maddened by yet another defeat, Kamsa took matters into his own hands. He hopped over the barrier and drew his sword with a delirious look in his unblinking eyes, and barreled towards Krishna. The vigilant Krishna, however, clocked the threat instantly, snatched up a nearby pole, and vaulted over Kamsa. Krishna then seized Kamsa by his hair, wrested the sword from his hands, and lopped off the king's head without so much as breaking a sweat. Finally, he ripped the conch off Kamsa's neck and sounded the horn in triumph.

The prophecy had been fulfilled.

It was only after Kamsa's death that Akrura disclosed to Krishna the truth about his parentage. With this revelation in mind, Krishna liberated Vasudeva and Devaki, as well as Ugrasena, from their prison cells and soon thereafter reinstated his maternal grandfather as King of Mathura. Now that Ugrasena had been restored to the throne, he resumed his reign, and wore the crown until the day of his death.

About a year or so after the completion of the prophecy, Rohini bore for Vasudeva another daughter named Subhadra, who, like her brothers, would go on to become a goddess in her own right. Unlike Krishna and Balarama, however, Subhadra was raised in the lap of luxury, and was thus a complete stranger to the modesty and strife associated with the life of a simple cow-herder. Subhadra later married her cousin Arjuna, whose mother, Kunti, was the sister of Vasudeva.

Krishna and Balarama did not return to Vrindavan. Instead, Vasudeva arranged for the brothers, along with their cousin Udhava (the son of Vasudeva's brother Devabhaga) to be relocated to Avantipura. There, they would reside in the dormitories of a prestigious spiritual center and academic institution, and receive a higher education from its operator, Sandipani Muni, for the next six years.

From his guru, Krishna was given intensive courses on the Vedas, Upvedas, and Upanishads, and the 64 traditional performing arts, or *Kala*, among which included g*eet vidya* (singing), *nritya vidya* (dancing), *alekhya vidya* (painting), and *sugandha-yukti* (the science of aromatics). A substantial portion of his education was devoted to the utilization and manufacturing of weapons. Krishna was found to be proficient in almost every weapon imaginable, but he had a special penchant for the throwing discus.

Krishna, who was immensely grateful for Sandipani's tutelage and friendship, urged him to set his own *dakshina*, a fee or offering typically donated to such an instructor. To Krishna's surprise, Sandipani rejected his gifts. There was only one thing he longed for: the return of his son, Punardatta, who had been kidnapped by Panchajana, the leader of the Punarjana tribe, the previous year. The Punarjanas were swashbuckling pirates who plundered precious gems, rare herbs, and other similar valuables from the villages they raided, which they sold for profit. The rest of their fortune was procured through the kidnapping of able-bodied men and maidens, who were then pawned off to the highest bidders.

Krishna, accompanied by Udhava, located Panchajana's ship a few weeks later. The daring duo climbed aboard the vessel, and upon coming face to face with the captain himself, demanded the release of their "brother" Punardatta. Unsurprisingly, Panchajana, who noted the intruders' lack of arms, cackled at his request, and ordered his men to toss the trespassers into wooden cages. Krishna's heart-stopping good looks were not lost on Panchajana, who was certain to fetch an equally handsome price.

Of course, these cages were, to put it generously, small potatoes for a man of Krishna's talents. He remained in voluntary captivity for several days, during which he befriended the ship's prisoners and crew – many of whom were captured by Panchajana and made to work as slaves themselves – and secured the location of the port where Punardatta had been unloaded. When Panchajana grew tired of Krishna's antics, he lunged at his blue-skinned captive, only to be thrown overboard by Hullu, one of his own bodyguards. Krishna, who assumed control of the ship, then steered the vessel towards Vyavashthapuri, rescued Punardatta from the clutches of the matriarchal overlords, and sailed back to Avantipura.

Following Punardatta and Sandipani's emotional reunion, Krishna headed back to Mathura, which was once again embroiled in a crisis. The long-awaited peace that prevailed following Ugrasena's return to the throne was short-lived. Rapacious rulers, in particular King Jarasandha of Magadha, interpreted the abrupt power transition as a sign of Mathura's fragility, and were keen to take control of the prosperous kingdom.

Legend has it that Brihadratha, the previous king of Magadha, had two wives who each gave birth to half a child – one missing its lower extremity, and the other lacking a head and upper torso. Disturbed by these anomalies, the castle servants discarded the incomplete and exanimate infants in the backwoods. Later that evening, a demoness named Jara who was stalking the hinterlands for animal carcasses happened upon the two halves. Once she pieced them together, the infant sprang to life; she then delivered this newly-formed baby to

Brihadratha, who compensated her with a princely reward for her troubles. This baby was none other than Jarasandha.

Jarasandha, who eventually inherited the throne, set upon Mathura not once, but 17 times. Fortunately for Mathura's citizens, Krishna, who served as the kingdom's premier general, thwarted every one of these attacks. Slowly, but surely, he annihilated all of the Magadha warriors until only Jarasandha remained.

Not long after, Krishna's five cousins, who rose to prominence as the heads of the Pandava clan, raised the new kingdom of Indraprastha. Yudishtra, the eldest Pandava, sought to carry out the *Rajasuya Yagya,* a consecration ceremony in which he would officially be recognized as the imperial overlord of Indraprastha and all her surrounding territories. Yudishtra, however, could not secure this title until Jarasandha was extracted from the equation, and as such, he turned to Krishna.

A strategy was devised. Krishna, Bheema (the second Pandava), and Arjuna (the third) donned brahman robes and ventured forth to Magadha, where they invited Jarasandha to partake in a wrestling match. Never one to turn down a challenge, Jarasandha took the bait, and chose Bheema as his opponent. Jarasandha and Bheema, who were evenly matched, tussled for four days straight.

When Krishna learned of Jarasandha's uncanny genesis, he took Bheema aside and clued him in to the new plan. Bheema tackled Jarasandha to the ground, detached the trunk of his body from his legs, and flung the halves in opposite directions. In return for the now vacant throne, Jarasandha's son, crowned the new king of Magadha, agreed to pay tribute to the Pandavas. A total of 88 kingdoms were also emancipated from Jarasandha's totalitarian authority.

Now, while the soldiers of Mathura, under Krishna's guidance, succeeded in foiling all of Jarasandha's invasion attempts, the kingdom sustained crippling losses from the rash of assaults. Krishna therefore persuaded Ugrasena and Vasudeva to abandon their battered headquarters and establish a new capital. A new city, christened "Dwarka," was erected, now believed to be the first capital city of what is now Gujarat.

In some accounts, Krishna and what remained of the Mathura citizens constructed Dwarka themselves. In other accounts, Krishna called upon Visvakarma, the architect of the demigods, to build him a new city. Visvakarma agreed to grant Krishna this favor under one condition: that Krishna pay his respects to Samudradev, god of the sea. Krishna was happy to indulge him, and in exchange, was allotted a dozen *yojanas* (roughly 299 square miles) of land.

The new metropolis, which was supposedly constructed in 48 hours, was a spectacular and futuristic work of art. The paradisaical complex, encircled by fortified sandstone walls, was split into six sections, and was furnished with spacious roads, colorful markets, aromatic gardens, artificial lakes, imposing amphitheaters, and anywhere between 700,000 to 900,000 opulent palaces trimmed with gold, silver, and crystal, and spangled with emeralds and other precious stones. Dwarka, akin to an island, was surrounded by the Arabian Sea; visitors from the mainland could only enter the city through the royal port or one of the bridges that linked the mainland to the city. It was here that Krishna remained for the rest of his days.

In Kundinapura, around 600 miles east of Dwarka, there lived a princess named Rukmini, who was the daughter of Bhishmaka, ruler of the Vidarbha kingdom. The ravishing raven-haired damsel was said to have been the most desired princess in all of India and was relentlessly pursued by a myriad of admirers. Despite her royal status, however, Rukmini, like most women, was robbed of the right to determine her own future. Her brothers had already arranged a companion for her: Prince Shishupala, hoping to secure a political allegiance with the Chedi kingdom. While a *swayamvara* – a ceremony wherein a maiden was made to choose her husband from a curated line of suitors – was to take place, it was merely a formality; Rukmini's fate had already been sealed.

Rukmini begged her brothers to stay out of her love life, but they would not be swayed. She had fallen in love with Krishna a few years prior, when he came to Kundinapura to mediate a dispute between the Pandavas and her brother, Rukmi. "I would faster throw myself down a well than marry Shishupala," said Rukmini. "There is only one man my heart belongs to, and his name is Krishna."

Rukmini discreetly dispatched a letter to Krishna, in which she professed her love for him, intimated her dilemma, and suggested that they engage in *rakshasa vivaha* (marriage by abduction). Moved by the princess' plight, Krishna took her up on her offer, and set a plan in motion. On the morning of the *swayamvara*, Krishna "kidnapped" Rukmini from the temple of Katyayani, and whisked her off on his chariot.

Krishna went on to marry seven other queens, altogether called the "*Ashtabharyas*": Satyabhama, Jambavati, Nagnajiti, Kalindi, Mitravinda, Bhadra, and Lakshmana. Rukmini bore nine sons, among them Pradyumna, believed to be the incarnation of Kamadeva, as well as a daughter named Charumati. Krishna's seven other wives also bore a brood of 10 children each.

Years later, Krishna freed 16,100 slave women from the lair of a demon named Narakasura. When their loved ones refused to welcome them back into their families, citing their sullied dignities, Krishna stepped forth and wedded every one of them to preserve their honor. As such, Krishna was a husband to 16,108 wives in total. Some insist that Krishna's unions with the 16,100 women were purely nominal, and that he never consummated any of these marriages. Conversely, conflicting accounts stated that they bore Krishna 160,000 sons.

Still, there remained a gaping hole in Krishna's heart that only one could fill. At this point, he had relinquished all hope of ever seeing Radha, his true love, again. But as the old sayings go – true love is patient, knows no distance, and never dies.

The childhood sweethearts may have been separated for decades, but the coruscating flames of Radha's love for Krishna had never faltered, and burned as brightly as the first day she met him. After the death of her husband, Radha, who was teetering on the brink of death herself – her skin now wrinkled and her hair a pearly silver shade – made the arduous trek to Dwarka, resolved to see her other half for the last time. She chose not to approach Krishna, and posing as a humble milkmaid, entered the *sudharma sabha* (the city hall), where Krishna was due to deliver a speech. Radha watched Krishna from afar, her heart swelling as she soaked in the details of his incredible new life.

Krishna's happiness was all that mattered to her, and seeing his bliss first-hand was all she needed. And with that, she started to head back to the place from whence she came. Unbeknownst to Radha, Krishna had spotted her in the crowd. He caught up to her near the city's gate, and following an extensive embrace, brought her to the prettiest lake in Dwarka. With her head nestled in his lap, Krishna serenaded Radha with her favorite song on his flute, tears streaming down his cheeks.

When Krishna played the final note, Radha's soul floated out of her body and merged with his, the two now bound together for all of eternity.

Ascension

"The only way you can conquer me is through love, and there, I am gladly conquered." – attributed to Sri Krishna

Over time, the Pandavas developed a turbulent relationship with their cousins, the Kauravas of the Kuru Kingdom. The estranged clans engaged in a bitter tug-of-war over the Hastinapura throne, the capital of the Kuru kingdom, which was at the time occupied by the Kauravas. The gradual disintegration of their relationship and the ensuing consequences of the animosity between the Indraprastha and Kuru kingdoms were captured in an epic now known as the *Mahabharata*, the 100,000 verses allegedly narrated to Ganesha by Krishna himself.

After several years of harrowing hostilities and needless suffering, the Pandavas made an attempt to mend the broken bridge between them and the Kauvaras. Krishna was appointed *Shanti Duta*, or "peace messenger," and sent to the Kuru court in Hastinapur on Yudhisthira's behalf. Krishna was reportedly such a beloved household name that he was greeted by a boisterous standing ovation upon his entrance.

Krishna addressed the Kuru prince, Duryodhana. The Pandavas, Krishna announced, were not seeking revenge, but rather, hoped to extend an olive branch to the Kauvaras. They only wanted what was rightfully theirs in the first place: the return of Indraprastha, or namely, half of the Kuru kingdom, which had been apportioned to them by Duryodhana's father, King Dhritarashtra. Yudhishtira, Krishna maintained, wanted nothing more than to end the family feud.

To Krishna's chagrin, Duryodhana spurned Yudhishitira's terms. He offered the prince an alternative: for the Pandavas to be granted ownership of five villages: Kusasthala, Makandi, Vrikasthala, Varanavata, and another village of Duryodhana's choice. Again,

Duryodhana repudiated his requests with disdain. Duryodhana puffed out his chest and declared that he would never award the Pandavas even a single acre of land, much less five villages. Krishna urged him to reconsider. By rejecting the Pandavas' conditions, Krishna warned, the Kauvaras will be met with a war of apocalyptic proportions.

As the legend goes, prior to what is now remembered as the "Mahabarata War" at Kurukshetra both Arjuna (on the side of the Pandavas) and the shameless Duryodhana petitioned Krishna for his help.

The day before the outbreak of the war, the rivals visited Krishna in the dead of the night and nudged him awake. Krishna promised that he would grant them each one of the following two: the *Narayani sena*, a powerful battalion consisting of 21,870 elephants, 21,870 chariots, 65,610 horses, and 109,350 infantrymen previously captained by Krishna, which played an instrumental role in the vanquishing of various invading forces; or Krishna himself, albeit not as a warrior, but rather, an adviser. As Krishna saw Arjuna first, the Pandava was granted first dibs. Arjuna chose Krishna, and requested that he serve as his personal charioteer; Duryodhana was given authority over the *Narayani sena*.

In the days leading up to the war, Arjuna was struck by cold feet, repulsed by the prospect of slaughtering his own kith and kin. Arjuna repeatedly sought counsel from Krishna and communicated his misgivings. Each time, Krishna told Arjuna not to lose sight of his cause and reminded him that it was his *dharma,* or duty to uphold righteousness and justice. The dialogue between them can be found in the *Bhagavad Gita,* one of the most treasured pieces of religious literature in the Hindu religion. Thus, the Kauvara Army, composed of 2,405,700 soldiers across 11 *akshauhinis* (units), faced off against 1,530,900 Pandava warriors.

The Pandavas, while vastly outnumbered, declared victory on the 18th day of battle. King Dhritarashtra was dethroned, and Yudhishthira was crowned king of Hastinapur. As a token of respect and goodwill, Krishna stopped by the chambers of Queen Gandhari, the consort of the blind Kauvara monarch and the incarnation of Mati, the goddess of intelligence, to inform her of his impending departure.

Gandhari was as vindictive as she was fiercely loyal. To provide some perspective, she voluntarily blindfolded herself on the day of her wedding and remained as such for the rest of her life, because, as *Times Now* contributor Gayathri Iyer explains, "she did not want to reap the fruits of vision that her husband was deprived of." When

Krishna solicited the queen's blessings, Gandhari leapt to her feet and inflicted upon him a dreadful curse, as she held him responsible for the deaths of Duryodhana and her 99 other sons – all of whom had perished in the war. Krishna, Gandhari snarled, would be doomed to endure the torture of outliving and losing his entire family, and witnessing the collapse of Dwarka and the disgraceful end of the Yadu Dynasty.

Interestingly enough, Krishna had the option to touch Gandhari's feet, for in doing so, the queen would be constrained to retract her curse. Krishna deliberately refrained from granting himself this immunity. Instead, he offered his sincerest apologies, bowed deeply, and retreated from her chambers. His heavy heart was laden with remorse. He may also have been saddled with the guilt of making the conscious decision to, in a sense, sacrifice the life of his nephew Abhimanyu, the son of Arjuna and Subhadra, who was only 16 when he was killed in battle.

See, Abhimanyu was the reincarnation of Varchas, the son of Chandra, the moon god. 17 years ago, Vishnu and a number of other *devas* sought Chandra's permission to send Varchas to the mortal realm. Chandra, who could hardly bear the thought of being apart from his son, agreed, but put forth the following stipulation: Varchas was only to remain on Earth for no longer than 16 years.

Some believe that the entire war had been orchestrated by Krishna. It was he who sowed the seeds of avarice and aggression in the Kauvaras, and he who incited the Pandavas' resentment towards their cousins – all to ensure the death of Abhimanyu. When Abhimanyu was still in the womb, Krishna temporarily endowed him with the ability to listen to and absorb the conversations between his parents. One day, Abhimanyu heard Arjuna describe the logistics of the *chakravyuha* to his mother, mainly how to best penetrate the discus army formation. Just as Arjuna began to launch into the ideal exit strategies, Krishna cut off the feed. When the Kauvaras assumed the *chakravyuha* formation on the 13th day of battle, Abhimanyu charged straight into the heart of the discus on his chariot. The teenager managed to butcher quite a few generals and high-ranking officials, but the circular wall of soldiers eventually closed in, and Abhimanyu, who could not find a means of egress, was ultimately overpowered and killed.

Gandhari's curse, much like the prophecy revealed to Kamsa, came to pass. In the decades that followed, Dwarka was rife with scandal, slander, selfishness, egotism, wickedness, and other forms of *adharma.* Just as Gandhari had foretold, Krishna lost all of his sons and grandsons to infighting, and the once time-honored Yadu Dynasty crumbled 36 years later.

Devastated by the loss of what was virtually his entire world, the inconsolable Krishna went to the forest by Somnath in Bhalka Teerath. There, he knelt down on the grass and closed his eyes, hoping to clear his head through meditation. Just minutes later, a passing hunter named Jara shot a poisonous arrow at what he interpreted as the eye of a deer, only to find out that he had struck the foot of the city's very own founding father. Incidentally, this was the same foot that had once been broken by a soldier named Barbarik a few years before the Mahabharata War. Upon realizing what he had done, Jara burst into tears and attempted to bandage Krishna's foot with a strip of cloth that he torn off his robe, but Krishna unwound the cloth, assured him that all was well, and forgave him.

It was an agonizingly slow and miserable death, characterized by loneliness and excruciating pain. He held on until February 18th, 3102 BCE, and was supposedly 126 years and five months old at the time of his death. Once he released his final breath, his soul ascended to the heavens, and his physical body vanished from the mortal realm shortly thereafter. Krishna, who had survived multiple wars and the most ferocious demons that the underworld had to offer, had been killed by a single arrow – and by accident.

All eight of Krishna's wives reportedly presented themselves as offerings, and threw themselves into a bonfire at their husband's funeral. Seven days after Krishna's death and disappearance, the whole city of Dwarka was swept away and submerged by a violent storm. A number of new cities were constructed on the land where the mystical capital once stood. Modern-day Dwarka is believed to be city number seven.

Krishna continues to be a ubiquitous presence – not only in India, but around the world – in the 21st century. Not only is Krishna one of the most prominent major deities in Hinduism, he is also a central figure in the Buddhist and Jain faiths. The *Krishna Janmashtami*, which falls on the *Ashtami,* or Krishna's day of birth, remains one of the most widely celebrated festivals in India today, during which Hindus engage in 24-hour fasting, present offerings of butter treats and milk sweets, and burn ghee-soaked candles at midnight.

It is only fitting to conclude with a prayer for Sri Krishna from *Sivananda Online*:

> "I bow again and again to Lord Krishna, son of Vasudeva, the delighter of Devaki, the darling of Nandagopa, the protector of cows...
>
> Teach me now the mysteries of Thy divine play and the secrets of Vedanta...

I recognize Thee alone as the mighty ruler of this universe and the inner controller of my three bodies...I trust Thee alone, O ocean of mercy and love! Elevate, enlighten, guide, and protect me.

Remove the obstacles on my spiritual path. Remove the veil of ignorance...”

Online Resources

Other Indian history titles by Charles River Editors

Other books about ancient history by Charles River Editors

Other titles about Krishna on Amazon

Further Reading

Aggarwal, V. (2017, December). 33 Devas. Retrieved September 8, 2020, from http://decodehindumythology.blogspot.com/p/suryavansham.html

Arora, P. (2017, August 14). In Search of Krishna in Vrindavan’s Secret Forest. Retrieved September 8, 2020, from https://www.arre.co.in/people/krishna-janmashtami-vrindavan-nidhvan-gopi-kanhaiyya-raas-leela-gokul/

Bachchan, A. R. (2017, August 14). WHY DID LORD KRISHNA MARRY RUKMINI IF HIS LOVE FOR

RADHA WAS SO DIVINE? Retrieved September 8, 2020, from https://www.beingindian.com/good-reads/why-did-lord-krishna-marry-rukmini-if-his-love-for-radha-was-so-divine

Basu, A. (2016, August 25). Mahabharata. Retrieved September 8, 2020, from https://www.ancient.eu/Mahabharata/

Bhatia, P. (2018). Existence of Lord Krishna – When the facts overshadowed the Myth. Retrieved September 8, 2020, from https://detechter.com/existence-of-lord-krishna-facts/

Caron, M. (2018). 10 Interesting Facts About Vishnu. Retrieved September 8, 2020, from https://blog.sivanaspirit.com/10-facts-about-vishnu/

Cartwright, M. (2012, November 25). Vishnu. Retrieved September 8, 2020, from https://www.ancient.eu/Vishnu/

Cartwright, M. (2015, October 1). Krishna. Retrieved September 8, 2020, from https://www.ancient.eu/Krishna/

Chanda-Vaz, U. (2017). Krishna and Rukmini: How His Wife Was a Lot Bolder Than Today's Women. Retrieved September 8, 2020, from https://www.bonobology.com/krishna-and-rukmini/

Chaudhary, A. (2018). 12 Beautiful Facts Of Radha Krishna Relationship. Retrieved September 8, 2020, from https://www.bonobology.com/radha-krishna-relationship/

Chopra, N. (2020, August). 11 Interesting Things About Krishna That Most People Don't Know. Retrieved September 8, 2020, from https://www.scoopwhoop.com/interesting-things-about-krishna/

Das, B. (2014, July 1). Radhe Krishna Story - The First Meeting of Radhe and Krishna. Retrieved September 8, 2020, from https://isha.sadhguru.org/global/en/wisdom/article/radhe-krishna

Das, S. (2019, July 25). 10 of the Most Important Hindu Gods. Retrieved September 8, 2020, from https://www.learnreligions.com/top-hindu-deities-1770309

Das, S. (2019, July 3). Who Is Lord Krishna? Retrieved September 8, 2020, from https://www.learnreligions.com/who-is-krishna-1770452

Das, S. (2019, June 25). The Birth of the Popular Hindu God Krishna. Retrieved September 8, 2020, from https://www.learnreligions.com/the-story-of-the-birth-of-lord-krishna-1770453

Dasa, S. (2016, July/August). The Dual Stories of Krishna's Birth. Retrieved September 8, 2020, from http://btg.krishna.com/dual-stories-krishna's-birth

Dey, N. (2017, June 1). Tales from Srimad Bhagavatam: The Birth of Balarama – XXVIII. Retrieved September 8, 2020, from https://www.differenttruths.com/relationship-lifestyle/religion/tales-from-srimad-bhagavatam-the-birth-of-balarama-xxviii/

Dixit, S. (2020, April 10). RUKMINI AND SHRI KRISHNA: The Abduction. Retrieved September 8, 2020, from https://medium.com/@Sanjay_Dixit/rukmini-and-shri-krishna-the-abduction-b8bdf843f861

Dixit, S. (2020, January 3). Why KRISHNA killed Kamsa: He could have been arrested and jailed! Retrieved September 8, 2020, from https://medium.com/@Sanjay_Dixit/why-krishna-killed-kamsa-he-could-have-been-arrested-and-jailed-a1550165850e

Editors, A. H. (2020). Who is Lord Vishnu and His 10 Avatars. Retrieved September 8, 2020, from https://www.asiahighlights.com/india/vishnu

Editors, A. L. (2017, August 10). The Symbolism Behind the Story of the Birth of Lord Krishna. Retrieved September 8, 2020, from

https://www.artofliving.org/wisdom/theme/symbolism-
behind-birth-of-lord-krishna

Editors, A. O. (2015, October 18). Dwarka: The Home
of Krishna is a Gateway to Heaven and an Underwater
City. Retrieved September 8, 2020, from
https://www.ancient-origins.net/ancient-places-
asia/dwarka-home-krishna-gateway-heaven-and-
underwater-city-004227

Editors, B. B. (2009, August 24). Who is Vishnu?
Retrieved September 8, 2020, from
https://www.bbc.co.uk/religion/religions/hinduism/deities/
vishnu.shtml#:~:text=Vishnu is represented with a,things
he is responsible for.

Editors, B. B. (2019). The existence of God. Retrieved
September 8, 2020, from
https://www.bbc.co.uk/bitesize/guides/zv2fgwx/revision/7

Editors, B. S. (2020, January 21). How Lord Krishna Got
His Name? Story Behind His Naming Ceremony.
Retrieved September 8, 2020, from
https://www.boldsky.com/yoga-
spirituality/anecdotes/2018/how-krishna-got-his-name-
122074.html

Editors, D. O. (2011). How Lord Krishna Killed Kamsa:
Story of Kamsa Vadh. Retrieved September 8, 2020, from

https://divine.onlineium.com/articles/how-lord-krishna-killed-kamsa-story-of-kamsa-vadh

Editors, D. T. (2018, September 19). Can science explain blue skin of Lord Krishna? Retrieved September 8, 2020, from https://www.downtoearth.org.in/news/health/did-lord-krishna-really-have-blue-skin--55392

Editors, E. C. (2019, September 12). Vishnu. Retrieved September 8, 2020, from https://www.encyclopedia.com/philosophy-and-religion/eastern-religions/hinduism/vishnu

Editors, F. P. (2017, October 10). Top 14 Lord Krishna Stories for Kids. Retrieved September 8, 2020, from https://parenting.firstcry.com/articles/top-15-childhood-krishna-stories-kids/

Editors, G. E. (2013). Dwarka, 12,000 Year Old City of Lord Krishna in Gujarat. Retrieved September 8, 2020, from https://www.gujaratexpert.com/dwarka-history/

Editors, H. K. (2017). - Salvation of Trinavarta -. Retrieved September 8, 2020, from http://www.harekrsna.de/artikel/Trinavarta-e.htm

Editors, H. T. (2019, August 23). Krishna Janmashtami 2019: The story of Lord Krishna's birth. Retrieved September 8, 2020, from https://www.hindustantimes.com/more-lifestyle/krishna-janmashtami-2019-the-story-of-lord-krishna-s-birth/story-4E62vFF3DszD9fwLMR7oPJ.html

Editors, I. P. (2017). The Story of Krishna and Jarasandha. Retrieved September 8, 2020, from https://www.indiaparenting.com/the-story-of-krishna-and-jarasandha.html

Editors, I. S. (2014, March 13). Krishna in Mahabharata – Treachery at Kurukshetra. Retrieved September 8, 2020, from https://isha.sadhguru.org/global/en/wisdom/article/krishna-in-mahabharata

Editors, I. S. (2014, May 20). The Birth of Krishna - Story of Krishna Janmashtami. Retrieved September 8, 2020, from https://isha.sadhguru.org/global/en/wisdom/article/krishna-birth-story

Editors, I. S. (2014, May 27). Butter Pranks - Krishna in Gokula. Retrieved September 8, 2020, from https://isha.sadhguru.org/global/en/wisdom/article/krishna-childhood-gokula

Editors, I. S. (2015, January 24). How Krishna Killed Kamsa. Retrieved September 8, 2020, from https://isha.sadhguru.org/global/en/wisdom/article/how-krishna-killed-kamsa

Editors, I. S. (2015, March 27). Krishna's Guru Dakshina: In Search of Pirates. Retrieved September 8, 2020, from https://isha.sadhguru.org/global/en/wisdom/article/krishnas-guru-dakshina-in-search-of-pirates

Editors, I. S. (2016, August 25). Krishna Stories: Exploring Krishna's Path of the Playful. Retrieved September 8, 2020, from https://isha.sadhguru.org/global/en/wisdom/article/krishna-stories

Editors, K. B. (2015, October 23). ROLE OF LORD KRISHNA IN KURUKSHETRA WAR. Retrieved September 8, 2020, from https://krishnabhumi.in/blog/role-of-lord-krishna-in-kurukshetra-war/

Editors, K. B. (2018, October 6). RADHA'S SEPARATION FROM KRISHNA: THE LESSER KNOWN STORY. Retrieved September 8, 2020, from https://krishnabhumi.in/blog/radhas-separation-from-krishna-the-lesser-known-story/

Editors, K. J. (2018). LORD KRISHNA'S DISAPPEARANCE. Retrieved September 8, 2020, from http://www.krishnajanmashtami.com/lord-krishna-disappearance.html#:~:text=a white serpent.-

,Disappearance of Sri Krishna,Krishna's spirit left for heaven.

Editors, K. K. (2014). 43. The Killing of Kaṁsa. Retrieved September 8, 2020, from https://www.krishnalilas.com/43-the-killing-of-kamsa.htm

Editors, K. V. (2014, September 24). Krishna and Balrama Fight With Wrestlers. Retrieved September 8, 2020, from http://krishnavasudeva.blogspot.com/2014/09/krishna-and-balrama-fight-with-wrestlers.html

Editors, M. K. (2016, April). Brief Timeline of Shri Krishna's Life. Retrieved September 8, 2020, from http://muneshkumarkella.blogspot.com/2016/04/life-sketch-timeline-of-shri-krishnas.html

Editors, M. O. (2016). The story of Subhadra. Retrieved September 8, 2020, from https://www.mahabharataonline.com/stories/mahabharata_character.php?id=55

Editors, M. R. (2004, May 9). The Lost City of Dwarka. Retrieved September 8, 2020, from http://mahabharata-research.com/about the epic/the lost city of dwarka.html

Editors, M. W. (2017, March 31). Krishna on Coins-(Part I). Retrieved September 8, 2020, from https://www.mintageworld.com/media/detail/3526-krishna-on-coins-part-I/

Editors, N. H. (2019, June 6). Know Why lord Krishna broke his flute and how Radha died? Retrieved September 8, 2020, from https://www.newsheads.in/lifestyle/news/know-how-radha-died-why-lord-krishna-broke-his-flute-article-33153

Editors, N. I. (2018, August 12). The mythical city of Dwarka. Retrieved September 8, 2020, from https://www.newindianexpress.com/lifestyle/spirituality/2018/aug/12/the-mythical-city-of-dwarka-1855600.html

Editors, N. W. (2014). Kurma. Retrieved September 8, 2020, from https://www.newworldencyclopedia.org/entry/Kurma

Editors, P. B. (2000, October 3). Krishna And Gurukula. Retrieved September 8, 2020, from https://www.purebhakti.com/teachers/bhakti-discourses/19-discourses-2000/204-krishna-and-gurukula

Editors, P. C. (2019, August 30). Know about the story of Lord Krishna's Gurudakshina to Sandipani Muni. Retrieved September 8, 2020, from https://postcard.news/know-about-the-story-of-krishnas-gurudakshina-to-sandipani-muni/

Editors, S. M. (2006, December 12). LORD KRISHNA OVERTURNS THE MILK CART KILLING DEMON SAKATASURA. Retrieved September 8, 2020, from https://www.sukanyasmusings.com/2007/12/lord-krishna-overturns-milk-cart.html?m=0

Editors, S. O. (2011). Prayer to Lord Krishna. Retrieved September 8, 2020, from http://sivanandaonline.org/public_html/?cmd=displaysection§ion_id=610

Editors, T. H. (2009, September 20). Endearing pranks. Retrieved September 8, 2020, from https://www.thehindu.com/features/friday-review/religion/Endearing-pranks/article16882597.ece

Editors, T. H. (2018, April 10). Brahma is humbled. Retrieved September 8, 2020, from https://www.thehindu.com/society/faith/brahma-is-humbled/article23496295.ece

Editors, T. N. (2009, May 25). Know why Shri Krishna never married Radha. Retrieved September 8, 2020, from https://www.timesnownews.com/spiritual/religion/article/know-why-shri-krishna-never-married-radha/596816

Editors, T. P. (2016). Lord Vishnu – Hindu Gods and Deities. Retrieved September 8, 2020, from https://www.templepurohit.com/hindu-gods-and-deities/lord-vishnu-hindu-gods-and-deities/

Editors, T. T. (2018, October 15). Story of the Birth of Lord Krishna. Retrieved September 8, 2020, from https://www.tell-a-tale.com/story-of-birth-of-sri-krishna/

Editors, T. T. (2019, March 24). Https://www.tell-a-tale.com/krishna-kills-putana-bedtime-story/. Retrieved September 8, 2020, from https://www.tell-a-tale.com/krishna-kills-putana-bedtime-story/

Editors, V. F. (2020, September 4). Goddess Rukmini – The First Wife of Lord Krishna. Retrieved September 8, 2020, from https://vedicfeed.com/rukmini-the-wife-of-lord-krishna/

Hariharan, S. (2020, May 9). What Happened after Krishna Died? Retrieved September 8, 2020, from https://www.icytales.com/what-happened-after-krishna-died/

Hariharan, S. (2020, May 9). What Happened after Krishna Died? Retrieved September 8, 2020, from https://www.icytales.com/what-happened-after-krishna-died/

Harshal. (2014, October 14). Death of Jarasandh. Retrieved September 8, 2020, from https://medium.com/thinking-aloud/death-of-jarasandh-ff9ec8551beb

Iyer, G. (2020, May 11). Here's why Gandhari cursed Lord Krishna after Kurukshetra war. Retrieved September 8, 2020, from https://www.timesnownews.com/spiritual/religion/article/know-why-gandhari-cursed-shri-krishna-after-the-kurukshetra-war/482093

Kalore, A. (2020, May). Lord Krishna. Retrieved September 8, 2020, from https://www.richmont.org/wp-content/uploads/2020/05/Lord-Krishna-AK.pdf

MANHARSHARMA. (2020, June 6). Deciphering the Deities of Hinduism. Retrieved September 8, 2020, from https://www.ancient-origins.net/history-ancient-traditions/hinduism-0013819

Mark, J. J. (2020, June 15). Bhagavad Gita. Retrieved September 8, 2020, from https://www.ancient.eu/Bhagavad_Gita/

Mukhopadhyay, S. (2019, August 15). Why Lord Krishna didn't help Abhimanyu in Mahabharata? Retrieved September 8, 2020, from https://medium.com/@swatisscet/why-lord-krishna-didnt-help-abhimanyu-in-mahabharata-dc13a14392b2

Nair, B. (2013, May 5). THE LEGEND OF KRISHNA: BALARAMA AND SUBHADRA. Retrieved September 8, 2020, from http://vipasana-vidushika.blogspot.com/2013/05/the-legend-of-krishna-balarama-and.html

Nair, B. (2014, February 15). Sages from the Hindu Scriptures: Rishi Garga or Garga Muni. Retrieved September 8, 2020, from http://vipasana-vidushika.blogspot.com/2014/02/sages-from-hindu-scriptures-rishi-garga.html

Pal, S. (2020, August 12). 5 Beautiful Lord Krishna Temples From Across India. Retrieved September 8, 2020, from https://curlytales.com/5-beautiful-lord-krishna-temples-from-across-india/

Panda, L. (2018, April 21). Story of Jarasandha – from Cradle to the Grave. Retrieved September 8, 2020, from https://blog.storymirror.com/read/skqiskon/story-of-jarasandha-from-cradle-to-the-grave

Pattanaik, D. (2017). Krishna, the wrestler. Retrieved September 8, 2020, from https://english.webdunia.com/article/hinduism-gods-goddess/krishna-the-wrestler-116081000003_1.html

Prabhupada, B. S. (1970). 11. Killing the Demons Vatsasura and Bakasura. Retrieved September 8, 2020, from https://krsnabook.com/ch11.html

Prabhupada, B. S. (2004). The Appearance of Lord Krishna. Retrieved September 8, 2020, from http://hansadutta.com/ART_WSP/mms2.html

Prabhupada, B. S. (2015). 22. Stealing the Garments of the Unmarried Gopi Girls. Retrieved September 8, 2020, from https://krsnabook.com/ch22.html

Prabhupada, B. S. (2015). The Stealing Of the Boys and Calves by Lord Brahma. Retrieved September 8, 2020, from https://back2godhead.com/the-stealing-of-the-boys-and-calves/

Prabhupada, B. S. (2018). The Perfection of Yoga: Pure Love of Krishna. Retrieved September 8, 2020, from https://back2godhead.com/the-perfection-of-yoga-pure-love-of-krishna/

Prabhupada, S. (2015). Krishna Kills the Great Python Aghasura. Retrieved September 8, 2020, from https://back2godhead.com/the-killing-of-the-great-python/

Rallapalli, M. (2015, November 24). Vishnu: The Savior, the Preserver, and the Protector. Retrieved September 8, 2020, from https://scholarblogs.emory.edu/rel100hinduism/2015/11/24/vishnu-the-savior-the-preserver-and-the-protector/

Samal, S. (2018, August 25). How was Balarama born? What is the story behind that? Retrieved September 8, 2020, from https://thesrinibash.wordpress.com/2018/08/25/how-was-balarama-born-what-is-the-story-behind-that/

Sethi, A. (2007, March 10). True legends? Retrieved September 8, 2020, from https://timesofindia.indiatimes.com/home/sunday-times/deep-focus/True-legends/articleshow/1746526.cms

Sethi, A. (2014, September 10). Salvation of Demon Trinavarta by Lord Krishna. Retrieved September 8, 2020, from https://iskcondesiretree.com/profiles/blogs/salvation-of-demon-trinavarta-by-lord-krishna

Shah, S. (2020, August 11). The Story Of Lord Krishna's Birth. Retrieved September 8, 2020, from https://thejaijais.com/blogs/sunitas-blog/the-story-of-lord-krishnas-birth

Sharma, R. (2016, August 24). How Krishna was transformed from a tribal deity to a supreme god in the Puranic tradition. Retrieved September 8, 2020, from https://scroll.in/article/814754/how-lord-krishna-was-transformed-from-a-tribal-deity-to-a-supreme-god-in-the-puranic-tradition

Simha, R. K. (2010, September). How science discovered the historical Krishna. Retrieved September 8, 2020, from https://www.esamskriti.com/e/History/Great-Indian-Leaders/How-science-discovered-the-historical-Krishna-1.aspx

Srivastava, S. (2016, September 15). Krishna Vs Brahma-Tale of Self Realization. Retrieved September 8, 2020, from https://shekharsrivastavaofficial.com/2016/09/15/krishna-vs-brahma-tale-of-self-realization/

Swami, R. (2013, November 15). Radhanath Swami on Trinavarta. Retrieved September 8, 2020, from http://radhanathswamiyatras.com/articles/vrindavan-articles/radhanath-swami-on-trinavarta/

Swami, R. (2013, October 25). Radhanath Swami on Name giving ceremony of Krishna. Retrieved September 8, 2020, from http://radhanathswamiyatras.com/articles/vrindavan-articles/radhanath-swami-on-name-giving-ceremony-of-krishna/

Swamiji, M. (2016, May 1). BRAHMA'S TRICK(ED).
Retrieved September 8, 2020, from
http://godivinity.org/brahmas-tricked/

Willis, A. (2017, August 14). Krishna Janmashtami
2017: Quotes, poems, wishes, messages and pictures.
Retrieved September 8, 2020, from
https://metro.co.uk/2017/08/14/krishna-janmashtami-
2017-quotes-poems-wishes-messages-and-pictures-
6847249/

Free Books by Charles River Editors

We have brand new titles available for free most days of the week. To see which of our titles are currently free, [click on this link](#).

Discounted Books by Charles River Editors

We have titles at a discount price of just 99 cents everyday. To see which of our titles are currently 99 cents, click on this link.